SANTA'S BLOODY TERROR

ERIC BLOOD

SANTA'S BLOODY TERROR

ERIC BLOOD

For Mom, Dad, Aunt Nette, and Gran, who helped make my Christmases as a youngster terrific.

And for my brother, who showed me lots of terrible horror movies that I definitely shouldn't have been watching at that age, which ultimately led to stories like the one you are about to read.

1

LAID UP FOR X-MAS

Well this sucks, Zack thought. He laid in the hospital bed, his right arm in a thick plaster cast, thinking about how unfair life was to have dealt him this blow. Christmas eve with a fractured wrist, with nothing to do but sit back and think about how the holidays sucked. At least this year.

And it was supposed to be so great, his thoughts continued. Nineteen years old and in the prime of your life. With an invitation to Carrie's Christmas party no less. Carrie's best friend, Nancy, was sure to be there. Recently single Nancy to be specific. And you're stuck in this damn hospital bed.

Zack knew that when it came to Nancy, his window of opportunity was small. She was every guy's dream. She had the looks and the personality (hell, she legitimately liked football, and not just in the fake "I'll pretend to like football until we actually become a couple – then it's no more sports for you" variety. She actually really liked it!). Her days on the open market would be short.

Zack looked over at the clock on his bedside table. 9:02.

Shit, the party's been going on for over an hour. She probably already met someone.

Dammit, why did you have to join in that stupid pickup basketball game? Never been injured in your life, and this is the time you picked to get crippled. And it was a dirty play no less!

Stop moping, he tried to tell himself. It was a bad break (both literally and figuratively), but the surgery went well, you'll get to go home tomorrow, and the doctor is confident that you'll have full mobility in your wrist once it heals and the cast comes off in a couple of months.

Yeah, well, that doesn't do me any good for tonight. And the doctor also never met Nancy Snyderman.

Oh god, I'll bet she's wearing those leather pants tonight...

Knowing this train of thought was going nowhere productive, Zack leaned over and grabbed his phone. He had plenty of songs stored on it, but he felt like listening to some Christmas tunes, determined to not let his current situation get him down. He went to his radio app and selected the "Holiday Tradition" station.

It's the most wonderful time of the year, he told himself with a grin as he waited for the first song to play. I'm not going to let this little snafu ruin my holiday.

But those pants, his mind wandered.

And then the music began, with Elvis Presley's voice coming out of his phone, singing "Blue Christmas."

Really, Zack thought. Of all the Christmas songs in the world, that's the first one to come on? Face it, this is just going to be a piece of shit holiday this year, and even the radio gods won't let you forget it.

Resigned to his fate, Zack leaned back, closed his eyes, and soaked in the melancholy Christmas tune. As he did so, the door to his room opened.

Can't I just be miserable in peace?

"How's everything going in here?" Zack opened his eyes to the angelic voice. Standing before him was a tall and extremely attractive female. She was wearing blue hospital scrubs with a white thermal underneath. Although her outfit was not form fitting, Zack could tell that she was in good shape. She looked to be in her mid-twenties. Her light brown hair was pulled back in a ponytail. She wore little to no makeup, and she didn't need any.

She was beautiful.

The newcomer smiled at Zack as if to acknowledge that she knew he found her appealing. "I'm Samantha, and I'll be your new nurse for the night." She walked over to his bed and checked the different devices hooked up to him.

Damn, she even *smells* wonderful, Zack thought as she stood over him.

Seeming content with her observations, Samantha took a step back and looked at Zack. "Okay, well if you don't need anything, I'll let you get some rest."

A grin formed across Zack's face. "Don't rush out on my account," he said through his smile. "I'm Zack, by the way."

Samantha returned the smile with one of her own. "Yeah, I got that part," she said, holding up Zack's chart as she did so. Zack felt the slightest bit of embarrassment, but it quickly dissipated, and he didn't really care anyway. He was too enraptured by the goddess standing before him.

"But I really should be going if you don't need anything," Samantha continued. "I do have other patients to check on, you know."

"You sure?" Zack said. I mean, how many of your other patients are going to be listening to cool Christmas tunes like I am?"

Samantha continued to grin at her patient. "I do enjoy some nice holiday music, and you are pretty cute," Samantha responded, "but some of my other patients have slightly more serious ailments than a broken wrist." She patted his leg lightly, her smile still present. "I'll be back to check on you in a little bit."

"I'll be here," Zack said as Samantha turned and left the room.

Maybe this won't be the worst Christmas after all, Zack thought.

NAUGHTY OR NICE?

Jared sat on his sofa, doing his best to calm himself down. The fabric he had used to sew his Santa Claus costume was very thin, and the spring that was protruding from the sofa was poking into his posterior. But he barely noticed. He was too keyed up about the night ahead.

Although he was nervous, Jared knew that tonight would be the night when Samantha realized that they were meant to be together. After all, it was destiny. It just needed a little push, that's all. Hell, he honestly couldn't understand why she didn't see it as clearly as he did, but sometimes that was the way things worked. He was more than willing to do his part to make her see things his way.

He glanced over at the clock on the large cardboard box that he was using as his side table. It was a little after nine o'clock. Samantha should definitely be at work by now. He'd been watching her for a few weeks now, so he knew her shift at the hospital always started at nine o'clock on Friday nights. He had wanted to follow her there tonight as well, just to be sure her typical schedule held. After all, it was Christmas Eve, so it was possible that schedules could have been funky for the holiday. But he had to get ready for the big evening, so he just didn't have time to keep tabs on her tonight. And besides, it was fate! She'd be there, he was confident of that.

He got up, the loose spring leaving a tiny hole in the seat of his red pants. He made his way to the bathroom, kicking various empty cans out of the way as he did so. He flipped on the bathroom light and took a look at himself in the mirror.

He knew his work would never be mistaken for Betsy Ross's, but he didn't think he did too shabby a job, if he did say so himself. He was clearly Santa Claus, there was no mistaking that. Sure, maybe he didn't look as put together as Santa typically presented himself, but that didn't matter. It was the thought that counted. And when Samantha saw him in his homemade Santa suit, that was sure to help seal the deal. Besides, those Santa suits in the store were a complete rip off! Why waste money when you could make a perfectly acceptable one at home?

This whole night was a stroke of genius, and Jared felt that everything was coming together. He was going to surprise Samantha at the hospital in his Santa suit, and she would see him for the great guy that he was. After all, who could be mad at Santa? And just in case she did still have any lingering doubts for whatever reason, it would be much easier to smooth things over at the hospital. She wouldn't be able to run away from him, because she was working. And she surely couldn't yell at him in a hospital. On Christmas Eve no less! This would definitely allow him the time to make his case for why they were destined to be together. If it even came to that.

Adjusting his suit just a tad, he took one last look at himself in the mirror and decided he looked good. He flipped off the switch and left the bathroom. He walked over to the sofa, picked up his Santa hat, and plopped it on his head. He headed towards the door, but abruptly stopped. "Can't forget my bags of goodies," he declared, holding up his index finger. He retreated to one of the corners of the small apartment and picked up two large trash bags that were nearly bursting open. He flung them over his shoulders, one bag for each side, and sauntered out the front door whistling "Santa Claus is Comin' to Town."

LET IT SNOW! LET IT SNOW! LET IT SNOW!

Zack's feeling of melancholy was creeping back in. Sure, he now had a super hot nurse taking care of him, and she seemed to even like him a little bit (did she really say he was cute?), but she wasn't in the room anymore, and it was back to Dullsville.

That's okay, he told himself. She'll be back. And you'll be more prepared this time. Now that you know your nurse is such a babe, you can better formulate your plan of attack.

Zack assumed Samantha was older than him, but she still looked to be fairly young. He guessed around twenty-five. So six years between them. That's not that much, he thought. What's six years in the grand scheme of things? Besides, it wasn't like he was still in high school or something.

You have to go for it, he told himself. If not, you may regret it for the rest of your life!

Okay, maybe it's not that serious, but what the hell. What do you have to lose? Someone that looks like her probably already has a boyfriend anyway.

So worst case, you'll make a slight fool of yourself and then it will be over with. But best case...

He was asking her out. It was decided. After all, it was Christmas. The time for miracles!

And then it suddenly dawned on him. What if he never got the chance? Sure, she said she'd be his nurse for the night, but there's no guarantee in that. She might get called away on an emergency or something, and he would get relegated to the fat old man nurse. Or maybe she just takes a while to make the next visit, and he would be fast asleep by then. After all, it was starting to get late. And Zack had no idea how long between visits nurses gave their patients.

I'm not missing out on Nancy Snyderman, only to be rewarded with the hottest nurse on Earth, only to then be thwarted on both fronts.

Time for a little adventure!

Zack sat up and spun himself around so that his legs dangled over the side of the bed. He was about to hop off of the bed, when he suddenly felt lightheaded. He paused, took some deep breaths, blinked a few times, and settled himself. No problem, he thought. Just have to remember to take it easy. Life threatening or not, you did just have surgery less than twenty-four hours ago.

Feeling more stabilized, Zack slowly eased off of the bed and onto his feet. He was grateful for the hospital socks that were provided to him, for he could tell the floor was cold even through the fabric that covered his feet. He stood up fully, taking his time to make sure he was in good enough shape for his little escapade. No more feelings of faintness, luckily. Feeling more confident, he took a few steps towards the door.

Not too bad, he thought. Just moved a little too quick when first getting out of bed. Just take your time, and you'll be fine.

It's not like you're going to running laps around the hospital or anything.

Feeling more sure of himself, he picked up his pace a bit and headed towards the door. But upon passing the window to his room, something caught his eye. He moved closer and peered outside. Was that snow he saw? He looked closer, determining that it was indeed winter precipitation falling from the sky. It's beginning to look a lot like Christmas, he hummed to himself. And your present is out there in the hospital somewhere!

With that thought, he made his way over to the door of his room. He stopped for a brief moment, thought about whether he should be leaving his room, and quickly decided there was no good reason not to head out in search of the object of his newfound infatuation.

He opened the door and headed into the hospital hallway.

HAVE YOU BEEN WORKING OUT, SANTA?

As Jared pulled his Ford Bronco into the snow covered parking lot, he was in great spirits. It had started to snow on the way over to the hospital, but it wasn't nearly bad enough to slow down his truck. Not that anything was going to stop tonight anyway, but still, he knew it was a sign from the heavens. A nice Christmas snow. Not enough to hamper his plans, but something to make the night even more magical. So far, everything was going perfectly.

He leaned his head down and looked at his face in the rearview mirror. Looking pretty good, he decided as he adjusted the hat on top of his head. Feeling good about his appearance, he pulled up the parking brake, turned off the ignition, and got out of the truck. He made his way to the bed of the pickup truck, reached in, and pulled out the two large trash bags, one in each clenched fist. They had some snow on them, but he didn't really care. He had thought about putting them in the back seat to avoid any damage being done to them, but he decided against that. He felt more like Santa this way, with his bags of goodies in the back of his sleigh. And a little snow wasn't going to hurt anything. If anything, it simply added to his Santa representation.

He started walking towards the front entrance of the hospital. This really was a stroke of genius, he thought. *No one can resist Santa. It's snowing, and I got my bags of goodies. And the most important thing, Samantha and I are meant to be together. What could possibly go wrong?*

He felt more confident with each step he took.

He arrived at the main entrance, knowing this was going to be the best night of his life. He was beaming.

Just like the real Santa Claus, he thought, and even let out a little "ho ho ho" of his own.

The automatic doors slid open, and Jared strode into the hospital. He took a few step into the building and stopped, surveying his surroundings. Although he had seen the outside of the hospital many times during his times following Samantha, he had never actually gone inside.

Seems pretty empty, he thought. *Guess no one gets sick at Christmas.*

Or just another good sign. Nothing to distract me and Samantha from getting together tonight.

It wasn't a huge hospital like something you would see on one of those TV dramas starring all of the good looking doctors. But it was still big enough to have a large and open lobby.

Okay, he thought. *Here you are. Time to get a move on.*

Carrying his bags at his sides, he walked forward, ready to begin his search for Samantha. He didn't know exactly where she would be, as he assumed her rounds would take her around to various locations of the hospital throughout the night. But he was confident that he would find her eventually. After all, he had all night. And it was meant to be.

He walked about forty feet before someone called out to him. "Excuse me, sir. Can we help you?"

Jared turned his head in the direction of the voice. To his right sat two women behind a desk. It appeared to be the reception area.

Jared was initially caught off guard. "Hmmph," he mumbled to himself. He hadn't expected this. Dressed as old Saint Nick, he had assumed he would have free reign of the place. Who would question Santy Claus?

And he knew he had been moving with a clear purpose and confidence. Isn't that what people said? If you act like you belong, people will believe it. Right?

But he quickly got over his initial surprise at the interruption. No problem, he told himself. You *do* belong here. Just have to check with the reception ladies. No reason to think they're going to give you a hard time.

Feeling better, he put on his best smile, puffed out his chest, and sauntered over to the reception desk. Two women sat behind the desk. One was a plump, middle aged black woman. He assumed she was the one that had questioned him. The other one was a white skinny girl playing with her iPhone. She didn't seem to have much interest in what was going on, other than whatever she was staring at a few inches in front of her face.

Why couldn't the skinny chick be the only one on duty tonight, Jared wished.

"Hi there," Jared said confidently to the black woman. It came out sounding like something from a game show host.

The woman squinted her eyes at him. "What can I do for you?" she asked.

"Isn't it obvious," Jared responded as he looked down at the bags he was clutching and his Santa suit. He looked back up at the woman, his most charming smile plastered on his face.

She didn't look charmed. She simply stared at him, squinting harder, not saying a word.

"I'm here to deliver some good cheer to the patients," Jared said, feeling his initial answer wasn't going over so well with the staring receptionist. But this one didn't seem to make much of an impression either, as the woman continued looking at him with obvious suspicion.

Jared tried to remain looking calm, but the silence was starting to make him nervous. Just as he was about to provide more details of why he was here, the receptionist broke eye contact and looked down at her desk. She ruffled through some papers before looking back up at Jared.

"I'm going to have to call someone," she said matter of factly. "I don't have anything here about a Santa coming into the hospital tonight."

Call someone, Jared thought. What the hell does that mean?

Nervous that his master plan, which had been going so well before this damn black lady started getting uppity with him, was beginning to spiral out of control, Jared knew he had to do something fast. "I'm confused," he said in the most sympathetic voice he could muster. "This is a hospital. Aren't people allowed to go visit anyone they want? I didn't think I would need to check in."

"You're right," the woman replied. "Normally, we would simply let visitors in to see whoever they wanted to. But not a muscle head with two big trash bags in a sloppy Santa suit. That raises flags."

Fuck, I overdid it, Jared thought. Should have just come in as my normal self.

But the Santa bit seemed like such a great idea...

Who has a problem with Santa? Apparently this black bitch.

Jared looked over to the skinny girl, hoping she may see things his way. But she was still playing away on her phone.

The black woman picked up the phone on her desk.

"Now look," Jared started, pausing to lean in and read the woman's name tag, "Wanda. I don't think we need to go to all the trouble of getting other people involved."

Wanda looked back up at him. Then she looked back down at the phone and started dialing.

"Who are you calling?" Jared asked nervously.

"Well," Wanda said, "I was going to call my supervisor to see if he had any information on a Santa coming in tonight. But I've decided to go right to security instead."

5

ON THE MOVE

No luck so far, Zack thought as he made his way through the hospital hallways. But at least it beat sitting around doing nothing in his hospital bed.

Zack had worked his way down to the ground floor, quickly surveying each of the five floors as he did so. The hospital was fairly deserted, with Zack only seeing two hospital employees during his travels. Neither of them paid much attention to him.

Zack decided he might as well head back up to his room, as there wasn't much going on here anyway, and he didn't want to be absent from his room when Samantha came back to check on him. But before heading back, he decided to make a pit stop at the cafeteria. No need to make this trip a complete waste, he thought.

Like the rest of the hospital, the cafeteria was empty. It was getting late, so they were closed for business, but anyone could still come and sit down if they so desired. And there was a row of vending machines along the far wall. He walked over, looking at the selection of goodies.

And then it struck him. "Shit," he muttered. He felt like an idiot. Here he was staring at the snacks in the machines, and he had no money on him. He did a quick scan of the floor, hoping for some loose change, but nothing caught his eye.

This trip really was a bummer, he thought. And with your luck, Samantha probably did already visit your room, and you weren't there. You were busy meandering around doing nothing and not even able to get a snack for yourself.

What if I really did miss her?

Zack didn't think he was gone long enough for that to happen. Why would she make another visit to his room so soon after checking on him the first time? But what if she did for some reason, and he was gone? Maybe she had to check on him quick because she had to run off for an emergency, and now she was going to be occupied with other patients all night, and he would never see her again. All because he was too impatient to just wait around like a normal patient.

He knew that whole scenario was ridiculous, but moved a little faster to the elevator all the same. No sense taking unnecessary chances.

Maybe I did miss her, his thoughts continued, but it will be for the best. Maybe she'll be pissed that I left my room and she'll have to discipline me.

Again, ridiculous thoughts. But more fun to think about than the other scenario.

Smiling, Zack made his way to the elevator and pushed the button for the fifth floor.

6

SOME CHRISTMAS LOVIN'

Holy shit this is the best Christmas ever, Randy thought as he pounded into Dr. Simpkins. Her skirt was pushed up around her waist, and her legs were wrapped around him as he thrusted in and out, her backside hitting the inside of the bathroom stall door. It rattled harder with each thrust.

"Give it to me, give it to me," Dr. Simpkins shouted, louder than Randy would have preferred, but not enough for him to care during the throes of ecstasy. "I need your sample now."

Being one of the lab workers in the hospital, Randy had to put up with this kind of sex talk from Dr. Simpkins. It was kind of weird and kinky, but he didn't really mind. And it was a small price to pay for a chance to make time with the hottest doctor in the hospital.

"Let me down and take me from behind," Dr. Simpkins suddenly said. This happened quite a lot with her. She was very demanding, even during the love making sessions when she was being the "submissive" one. Whatever was taking place, she was always the one in control. And sometimes, like in this instance, she would want to change positions very abruptly. Whatever suited her tastes at that moment.

And Randy was happy to oblige.

Randy slid the doctor off of his glistening member and lowered her to the floor, her high heels clicking on the tile floor of the bathroom as she landed. She placed her hands on the toilet in front of her, bent her head down, and raised her ass in the air. Her skirt had remained above her hips, but her long white jacket had fallen back down. She pulled it up on to her back.

"Fuck me. Now," she demanded. Randy didn't hesitate, sliding his erection into her slick vagina. He placed both hands on her hips and began to pump away.

"Harder, faster," Dr. Simpkins commanded. They had already been at it for about twenty minutes, so Randy didn't have to be told twice. He was ready to blow.

"Oh fuck, give it to me now. Now!"

And Randy did. "Oh shit," he exclaimed as he exploded insider of her. Dr. Simpkins moaned, and rubbed her backside against Randy's groin. The last of his semen finally spurting out, Randy pulled back and out of the good doctor.

Breathing heavily, Randy leaned back against the door of the stall. "Jesus Christ, that was great," he said through deep breaths.

Dr. Simpkins pulled off a long roll of toilet paper, wadded it up in a ball, and wiped her private area clean. She then bent down, grabbed the panties that had fallen down around her ankle, and pulled them up. Once in place, she pulled down her skirt and did her best to smooth it out.

"It was adequate," she said, not looking at Randy as she continued adjusting her outfit.

Good grief, Randy thought. Sure, the sex is fantastic, and she's smoking hot, but why does she always have to be such a bitch.

Randy reached down and pulled up his own pants. Wearing

scrubs, he didn't have much to adjust. He opened the door of the stall, and they both exited into the main area of the bathroom.

Randy went over to the sink and began washing his hands. "Well, I guess I better get back to the lab," he said as he rinsed off. "I'm the only one on duty tonight, so I can't be gone for too long."

Dr. Simpkins began washing her hands as well. "Yes, I'm well aware of that. Maybe next time, you can take care of me a little faster so you don't have to worry about that."

"Well maybe if you didn't have to keep ordering me around and wasting time with your kinky nonsense, I wouldn't need so much time to 'take care of you.'" He regretted the words as soon as they came out of his mouth. But he had been dealing with her bad attitude for long enough, and he could no longer just take it.

Dr. Simpkins glared at him through her stylish, dark rimmed glasses. Her mouth opened the slightest bit as if she intended to say something, but she quickly closed it. She turned and started towards the door.

Fuck, Randy thought.

"Wait, I'm sorry," Randy said, chasing after her. He reached out and touched her arm, causing her to stop and spin around to face him.

"Don't touch me," she spat, jabbing her index finger into his chest. "Unless I tell you to. And if you ever talk to me like that again, I'll have your ass out of this hospital so fast, your head will spin."

Randy said nothing, knowing that nothing could come out of his mouth to help the situation at this point.

"Now," Dr. Simpkins said, drawing her finger down his torso and speaking in a much friendlier tone than just seconds before, "if you want to get back in my good graces...which you do if you want to remain employed...then you'll stop by my office after your shift." She then leaned in and kissed him. It was a sensual kiss, her tongue slowly working its way into his mouth, massaging his tongue. He started to reciprocate, and she pulled away from him.

"The sex tonight was good," she said, "but I'm not as satisfied as I need to be. You'll remedy that situation when you come to see me later." And with that, she patted his crotch and sauntered out of the men's room.

Randy stood still for a moment, not sure what exactly he was feeling. But, knowing he really did need to get back to work, he splashed some water on his face, dried himself off with a paper towel, and followed his lover out of the bathroom.

IT'S A DIRTY JOB, BUT SOMEONE HAS TO DO IT

Laymon Memorial Hospital had once been a great place to work. Sure, it had its issues, just like anywhere did. But overall, Samantha truly enjoyed coming to work and loved what she did. It was a relatively small hospital in a relatively small town, but it still had all of the modern amenities needed to care for the patients. It was the best of both worlds. Excellent treatment for the patients along with the attention and care that they deserved.

But those days were quickly vanishing.

Samantha took a seat on the bench outside of the linen closet. She looked at the cart full of supplies that still needed to be distributed and put away. She puffed out a breath and slouched down where she was sitting.

What a bunch of bullshit, she thought.

Samantha didn't mind helping out, that was for sure. And she knew damn well that there was more to being a nurse than just the exciting moments and saving people's lives (although it was pretty damn exciting, and she was involved with saving quite a few lives during her tenure at the hospital). But she didn't appreciate the tasks that continued to be piled on to her plate, as well as the plates of all the other nurses.

And it wasn't the tasks themselves that bothered her. It was the fact that it took time away from the patients that she should be checking on.

The hospital sure as hell wasn't willing to hire additional people that could help with these types of tasks, and they wouldn't even hire new nurses if anyone ever left the hospital. Rather, the staff that they were able to retain was expected to simply pick up the slack.

And so far, Samantha had been willing and able (at least for the most part) to do it. But lately, it had been getting harder.

She was burnt out.

Okay, maybe not officially burnt out, whatever the technical definition of that was. But she was definitely approaching it at a rapid pace. At the very least, her candle had melted down quite a bit and the wick was losing its flame quickly.

Yeah, well, the pile of bills on the counter doesn't really care about how tired you are, so better get a move on!

Sighing, Samantha pushed herself forward and stood up. "Let's see," she mumbled to herself as she looked at her cart, determining where she was headed next. "Ah, yes. The lab."

The wonderful, fucking lab.

Samantha began pushing the cart to her next destination. This was the shit that made her maddest of all. It was bad enough that they didn't have enough staff for the hospital, the important aspects of the hospital anyway, to run smoothly. But when it came to the lab, all bets were off. It seemed as though no expense was too much for the ever loving lab. Anytime there was a meeting, it was to update the staff on the lab. Every email was about new developments somehow related to the lab. The lab, lab, lab.

Fuck the lab, she thought.

Honestly, she wasn't even sure exactly what they did there. Some type of experimental drug development, she presumed from skimming over the emails and literature the hospital provided on it, but the details escaped her.

Something to make the drug companies and other corporations happy. And rich.

At the expense of actual patients.

Fuck the lab.

Maybe I shouldn't be quite so hard on it, she thought as she turned the corner with her cart. She understood that the hospital needed to make some revenue in order to stay in business. But she didn't understand why they needed to make record profits every year, while it seemed like the basic functions of the hospital suffered.

That wasn't true. She did understand.

People were greedy bastards.

Stop being a grump, she told herself. Sure, the world sucks, and people are jerks.

That's the way it always has been and probably always will be. But you have a job, and again, the pile of bills at home really doesn't care about your ideal thoughts of how the world should work. So get to work and stop complaining.

She continued to push the cart towards the lab.

JARED LOSES IT

Jared sat in one of the chairs facing the reception desk, his head in his hand, and his Santa hat precariously perched atop his head. His initial instinct had been to run out of the hospital as soon as Wanda said she was calling security, but he quickly nixed that notion. If he ran out now, he definitely wouldn't see Samantha tonight, and who knew when another opportunity would present itself.

No, he had spent too much time planning on tonight to give up on it so quickly. So things weren't going as smoothly as he anticipated. That was okay. The truly great things in life didn't come easy.

He would stick to the plan. He was Santa, and he was coming to deliver good cheer to the patients of Laymon Memorial Hospital. This Wanda bitch was just being an asshole. She probably did this to everyone. The security guards would probably come and laugh the whole thing off because she did this kind of thing all the time.

Yeah, she was probably known across the whole hospital as being a total bitch.

Nothing to worry about.

Still, Jared was getting more anxious waiting for security to arrive.

How long has it been, he wondered. Probably only a minute or so. It just seems like it's taking long because you're getting worked up.

Settle down. Everything will work out.

Remember, this is meant to be!

Feeling a bit calmer, Jared heard footsteps coming from down the hallway. He looked up to see a security guard turn the corner and begin heading toward him and the receptionists. He appeared to be alone.

Only one guard, Jared thought, his optimism rising. They can't think this is too serious if they only sent one guy. It really is what you were thinking before. They have to send someone out, since this bitch Wanda called for help, but they know she's just a retard that blows everything out of proportion.

Jared smiled. Everything was going to be fine.

The security guard walked over to the reception area and stopped. "Hey, Wanda," he said. He looked over to the skinny girl, but she was still wrapped up in whatever it was she was doing with her phone. He turned to Jared.

"Okay, what seems to be the problem here?"

"Well," Jared said as he started to stand. "As I was telling Wanda here..."

"Did I tell you to get up?" the security guard barked. "Sit back down."

Jared complied with the unexpected command from the guard. Not going quite as well as I hoped, he thought. He sat back down.

The guard turned his head, now looking directly at Wanda. "Okay, tell me the situation here."

"Well, 'Santa' here," she began, glaring over at Jared, who was looking guiltier by the second, "said that he's here to spread good cheer or some such bullshit. But I don't have any record of a Santa coming in tonight. And whenever we do have a Santa come around, they don't usually come at nighttime. And then he started acting weird on top of it, so I thought I better call you."

The guard looked back to Jared. "Well? Do you have anything to add?"

Jared looked up at the guard. He could feel Wanda's glare boring into him, and his eyes darted over to her. He glanced at the white girl, but she was still paying no attention to any of this. He was beginning to sweat under his red suit.

"Hello, Earth to Santa," the guard said, louder than before. "Are you supposed to be here or not? Do you have any identification?"

This is not going the way it was supposed to!

Jared's mind began racing. How did everything turn to shit so fast? He didn't expect anyone to actually question his presence at the hospital. This kind of thing never happened in the movies.

You've come too far, he thought. Planned too much to simply go home empty handed now.

But what could he say?

"Okay, buddy, let's go," the guard said as he walked over to Jared. "I'll even help you carry your trash out with you."

"It's not trash," Jared spat angrily. "They're my bags of goodies, and they're not for you."

"Whatever," the guard responded, seemingly not interested in what the contents of his bags was. He reached down and grasped Jared's arm.

It all happened before Jared even had a chance to think about it. As the guard was reaching down to grab him, Jared spied the gun in the guard's holster. Without contemplating what he was doing, only knowing that this pig was thwarting his rendezvous with Samantha, his hand darted out and latched on to the weapon. With a quick jerk of his arm, Jared relieved the guard's holster of its weapon, and he stood up out of the chair, pushing the guard away from him.

"Whoa, whoa," the guard said, holding his palms out towards the now armed Jared. Jared took one step forward, leaned towards the guard with his arm outstretched, and pushed the muzzle of the gun firmly into the guard's forehead.

The guard opened his mouth slightly as if about to speak, but he never got the chance. Jared pulled the trigger, causing the back of the guard's head to explode in a spray of red.

Screams came from behind the reception desk. Jared turned towards them, his arm remaining ramrod straight. The skinny girl was no longer holding her phone, and she was screaming endlessly. Wanda was no longer making any noise, but rather looked shocked at what she had just witnessed.

"So now you're paying attention," Jared said to the screamer.

She didn't stop.

Jared walked closer to the desk and shot her in the face. Unlike the security guard, this girl's entire head seemed to come apart. Jared wasn't sure if it was the placement of the bullet or if maybe she wasn't put together as well as the male guard. But either way, the screaming had ended.

Okay, this isn't going exactly as planned, Jared thought, but at least I'm not getting thrown out of the hospital anymore. There's still a chance for success tonight. I can find Samantha, she'll see that we belong together, and we'll simply be on our way. Might have to make some adjustments to the plans for after tonight, but we can adapt.

He turned to Wanda. "Why couldn't you have just let me in?" he said, grinning.

Wanda took a breath. "I think it's pretty obvious that my judgment was correct." She looked over her shoulder at the dead girl on the floor. She then leaned forward a bit, looking over the counter at the dead security guard.

Jared couldn't help but snicker at Wanda's comment. "Maybe you're right," he said. "Although if you had just let me through, this wouldn't have happened. So really, this whole thing was your fault."

Wanda stared at him, unimpressed. "Regardless, I still can't let you through. But you're free to leave from where you came. I can't do much to stop you at this point."

What's with this lady?

"Sorry, but I don't think there's much you can do to stop me from going in there, either. And I have no intention whatsoever of leaving. Not until I got what I came for. And you know I can't just leave you here, either. You'll call the cops, and in a few minutes, I'll be screwed."

"Yeah, that's probably about right."

"Well, in that case, I think you can understand why I need to do this."

Jared fired the weapon one more time; however, his aim was not as good as the previous two shots. He had aimed for Wanda's head, but instead hit her in the middle of her throat. A large red opening appeared under her chin, and blood began shooting out in spurts. Wanda's hands both went to the wound, but there was nothing that could be done to stop the blood flow. It continued to spurt, coating her hands. She gurgled and gasped as she slowly died. Her hands fell to her sides, and her body slowly crumpled off of her chair and to the floor. A few moments later, she lay still.

That wasn't what I intended, Jared thought. I was kind of starting to appreciate your sassiness by the end. Wanted to give you a clean death. My Christmas present to you, as it were.

"Oh, well," he said, shrugging his shoulders.

Time to get to the business at hand.

9

JINGLE BELLS THEY WERE NOT

Samantha was just about to push the button for the elevator when she heard the gunshots.

"Jesus Christ," she shouted involuntarily as she jumped, bumping into her cart and knocking some towels to the floor.

What the hell was that?

She turned around, looking in the direction that she thought the loud noise had come from. Her heart was slamming in her chest as she tried to listen for any other noises that were out of the ordinary. Leaving her cart behind, she crept down the hallway.

Was that screaming she heard now?

As she strained to hear what was happening elsewhere in the hospital, the second gunshot sounded.

"Holy fuck," she shouted, jumping backwards and putting her hands over her ears.

With the first one, she had tried to tell herself it could have been anything. But she now felt confident that they were both indeed gunshots.

She took her hands away from her ears, listened.

She no longer heard any screaming.

Samantha pulled her phone from her pocket and swiped her finger across the screen. She was about to dial security when the third gunshot sounded, causing her to drop her phone. It clattered on the tile floor.

She quickly reached down and picked up the phone. Please work, she mentally pleaded as she tried once again to activate it. It seemed to still be functioning properly, but she was not getting a signal.

"God fucking dammit," she said through clenched teeth. *Why can't I ever get a signal in this fucking hospital?*

Probably all of that fucking shit they're doing in the lab. Some kind of radioactive waves or something emanating throughout the whole first floor!

Okay, now you're just being stupid, she told herself. But either way, you need to figure out what to do.

Don't want to head back upstairs, she thought. As much as you want to get away from whatever is happening down here, if you go upstairs, you'll be trapped if the gunman follows.

Gunman? Is this really happening?

Sure as hell sounds like it, she thought. Why the hell not? Seems to be some type of shooting every day. Why not add Laymon Memorial Hospital to the list?

And even if you could find a way to escape, you can't just leave all of the patients and coworkers to fend for themselves. No, you need to figure out what's going on and get some help if possible.

At least the gunshots seem to have finally stopped.

She expected to be startled by another one as soon as that thought entered her head. But nothing came.

Not sure exactly what her plan was, she quietly moved towards the stairs that would take her to the first floor. And the hospital entrance.

JESUS FUCKING CHRIST, what was that!

Zack almost fell to the floor when the first gunshot rang out. He hadn't felt unsteady at all since initially getting out of bed, but explosions going off in the background surely didn't help anything.

By the time the third gunshot rang out, he was ready to pee his pants.

What the fuck's going on around here? I thought this was a hospital, not a warzone.

Were those even gunshots? Sure as hell sounded like it, but what do I know? You're experience with guns is watching the Die Hard movies.

Maybe that's not so far off. After all, it is Christmas, and something bad seems to be going down.

Should have just stayed in your room!

Yeah, and what good would that have done? The gunmen would still be here, and you'd be stuck up on the fifth floor. You may not have been able to track down Samantha, but you may have inadvertently saved your hide!

Yeah, right. You don't really know where you are in the hospital (I think the third floor?), and you don't know exactly where the gunshots (if that is even what they were) came from. But wandering around the hospital looking for nurse hottie, you could have just doomed yourself sooner.

Bottom line, Zack decided, is that he didn't know what the hell was going on.

And there's only one way to find out (and possibly get the hell out of here as well).

Time to investigate.

Hell, maybe you'll end up saving Samantha from the bad guys, and you'll be a hero. And more importantly, she'll be in your debt.

Or, he thought, you could focus on simply surviving the night.

10

OH, SHIT!

Samantha checked her phone one more time as she neared the hospital entrance, but there was still no signal.

Either this phone is a piece of shit or the hospital is in a dead zone.

Maybe the *dead zone.*

Part of her wanted to turn around and run the other way. Find a nice place to hide and wait things out. Someone else must have heard the shots and already called the police. Just go find a quiet nook of the hospital and wait for the cavalry to arrive.

But what if everyone thinks the same thing? What if everyone else is having phone issues as well?

What if everyone else is dead?

Now your imagination is getting the best of you, she told herself. There were only three gunshots (if that was even what they were). Everyone in the hospital isn't dead. At most, three people. Maybe four if the gunman is an expert marksman.

Way to make yourself feel better about things, Sam!

Enough, she told herself. You'll never figure out what's going on by just standing here being a wuss. Maybe there's something you can do to help, but you have to keep moving.

She started to creep forward again, staying as close to the wall as she could. She was just a few feet from an intersection in the hallway, and once around the next corner, she should be able to see the reception desk. She still wasn't positive, but she thought the noises came from that area. And if not, Wanda and the skinny girl (what was her name again?) should at least know what's going on. Or at least provide some clues.

Wanda, anyway. That skinny girl was kind of useless.

Samantha crept closer to the intersection. Her heart was beginning to beat faster. She feared what she would see when turning the corner. Although happy to not hear anymore gunshots, the silence was not much better.

She took another step closer.

Good god, what are you doing? Get the hell out of here!

She took a deep breath, held it. She took another step, now just inches away from the corner of the wall. She slowly let our her breath, careful to be as quiet as possible. She poked her head around the corner.

It was still a fair distance away, but she could see the reception desk from where she stood, and everything looked normal. She could clearly see two people sitting behind the desk, and it looked like Wanda and the skinny girl. They didn't seem to be doing much, not that Samantha would expect much activity at this time of night under normal circumstances. But when three loud noises that sounded like gunshots rang through the hospital, she would expect there to be some activity.

Did you *imagine* the noises, Samantha started to question herself, but quickly dismissed that notion. No, she definitely heard something. She couldn't be positive where it came from, but she heard something. And it was loud enough that the women at reception would have heard it too, wherever it originated from.

Samantha turned the corner and began walking towards the reception desk, looking around the lobby as she did so. Nothing seemed out of the ordinary at first glance, but something just felt off. As the distance between her and the front desk narrowed, Samantha felt more uncomfortable. Wanda and the skinny girl didn't appear to be moving at all.

Are they sleeping, Samantha wondered briefly, but this thought was quickly dismissed as she saw their faces more clearly. Or rather, as she saw *Wanda's* face, with her vacant stare and frozen look of agony. The skinny girl's face was no longer there, her head half missing and gore spilling out of it. Both of the women had been propped up on their swivel chairs, but both were clearly dead.

She heard the sound of a door swinging open to her right. She turned her head, feeling like her heart had stopped.

Out of the men's room came Santa Claus. But although he was whistling "Let It Snow! Let It Snow! Let It Snow!," this was clearly not the Santa Claus that she was told about when she was a little kid.

The man in the Santa suit was looking down at his hands as he wiped them off with a paper towel from the men's room. Content with his work, he let the towel fall to the floor and looked up. He stopped when he saw Samantha looking at him.

"Jared?" The words escaped from Samantha's lips in a mumble. *What have you done?*

Jared smiled.

Stay calm, Samantha told herself. Maybe it's not what it looks like. Maybe your ex-boyfriend didn't become a deranged Santa Claus and murder two of your coworkers.

"Jared, what the hell's going on?" she forced herself to speak.

"Oh my god," Jared said as he began walking towards her.

"You're more beautiful than ever. If I ever had any doubts about this, seeing you here now took care of that." As he moved closer, Samantha noticed the gun sticking out of the front of his pants. He also had speckles of blood on his face.

Okay, scrap any thoughts of him not being responsible for this.

"Now listen," Jared started again as he continued forward. "There's been a slight change of plans." He glanced over at the two corpses. "I had some interference that I wasn't expecting, so I had to improvise."

"Hold on a second," Samantha said, trying not to sound too rattled. Jared had clearly flipped his lid, and she didn't want to say anything to set him off. "What exactly did you have planned, and what happened here tonight? And why are you dressed like Santa?" She pretty much knew the answers to her questions, but she was stalling for time, trying to figure out the best course of action.

Jared looked down at himself and chuckled. "Yeah, in retrospect, I guess the Santa suit was kind of dumb. I didn't think anyone could resist Santa Claus. And I thought you would appreciate the effort."

He looked back up at Samantha. "And I can explain everything else to you later. The main thing is that I came to get you so that we can spend the rest of our lives together. And we really should be going," he said as he looked down at his wrist that didn't appear to have a watch on it. "I propped up the two dead bitches in their chairs, but I don't know how long that can fool people. And the dead security guard that I lugged into the bathroom stall won't keep forever, either."

Oh, god, Samantha thought. He really has lost it.

Jared could see that Samantha wasn't as impressed with his efforts as he thought she would be. "Wait, I almost forgot about my bag of goodies," he declared as the thought struck him. He jogged over to the two trash bags that he had left over by the reception desk. He picked them both up effortlessly and brought them closer to Samantha before plopping them back on the floor. They were both now coated with blood from the triple murder, and drops of red fluid flew from the bags upon impact with the floor.

"We can't forget our Christmas presents now, can we?" he said as he joyfully opened up one of the bags and stuck his hand in. He looked up at Samantha. "Have you been a good girl this year?" he said, really getting into character at this point.

Samantha stared at him, not sure how to answer.

"Oh well, doesn't matter," Jared said. "Let's see what Santa has for you." He peered into the bag and rooted around, looking for the perfect selection. "Ah, here we go," he said as he pulled out his prize, a huge smile on his face.

"Holy shit, what the hell is that?" Samantha exclaimed, involuntarily taking a step back from the demented Santa Claus. But she knew what it was. It was a human arm.

Jared looked at the gift he was offering. "Oh, I see why you're confused," he stated. "Obviously, it's an arm. But it's not just *any* arm. Here, let me get something better for you which should make it clearer." He threw the limb aside and started rooting around the garbage bag some more. His tongue stuck out slightly as he felt around determinedly.

"Here we go," he shouted, his eyes wide with the anticipation of presenting the perfect gift to his beloved. He pulled out the decapitated head, a huge smile plastered across his face.

Samantha stared at the head, aghast.

Jared looked at Samantha, clearly waiting for a positive reaction to his holiday offering. He looked back and forth between the head and Samantha, almost willing her to understand what he had done for her.

"Well," he finally said. "What do you think?"

"What have you done?" Samantha asked, not truly wanting an answer.

She got one anyway. "What do you mean?" Jared responded. "Don't you know who this is?" he continued, looking at the corpse's head.

Samantha kept staring at the grisly sight. In fact, she did not know who it was. Even if the head had not been rotting for who knew how long, she wasn't sure she would have recognized who the head had once belonged to.

Clearly frustrated, Jared piped up again. "I'll assume you're just a bit flustered by my unexpected appearance, so I'll help you out. It's that asshole mailman that's always harassing you. I've seen him coming to your house practically every day?"

"He's the mailman," Samantha said. "Of course he's going to come to my house every day. That's his job."

"Bullshit. I've seen the way he looks at you. Now you don't have to worry about him anymore."

Samantha started backing away some more. This isn't good, she thought. No, not good at all.

"Wait," Jared said. "We didn't even get to the second bag yet. Don't you want to see what else I brought for you?"

Samantha turned and sprinted back into the heart of the hospital.

11

INTO THE LAB WE GO

I can't believe this is happening, Samantha thought as she ran away from her ex-boyfriend. Apparently, her psychotic, murdering ex-boyfriend.

Check that, not even really an ex-boyfriend. More like an ex-guy you dated a tiny bit.

Well, apparently you had quite the effect on him!

As she ran, Samantha's mind raced along with her, thinking of what her next move should be.

You're pretty quick, she thought. But not sure if you're able to outrun Jared. And you definitely can't outrun a bullet.

Although he seems pretty smitten with you, so hopefully you won't be his directed target.

Yeah, and based on what you've seen so far, it's a real good idea to try to figure out his motives and stability. He's obviously a nutso!

Regardless of whether he plans to kill you or not, Samantha decided, the most prudent course of action at this time would be to get the hell away from him. She had just come from the main exit, so that wasn't an option. And she didn't want to head up to the higher floors if it could be helped. She'd seen enough movies with homicidal maniacs running around to know that wasn't usually a good idea. But where else should she go?

It suddenly hit her. The lab.

That's right, she thought as she started sprinting once again down the hallway. *The fucking lab is going to save your life. It needs an access card to get in, and the hospital big shots are always bragging about its security. Apparently, it has bullet proof glass and everything.* That had always annoyed Samantha previously, as she wondered what the hell they were working on in there to need unbreakable glass.

Who cares, she now thought. *As long as it keeps psychos out, it works for me.*

She skidded to a stop as she came to the next hallway intersection. She quickly glanced over her shoulder to see if she was being pursued.

No sign of Jared.

But she wasn't about to wait around for him to make an appearance.

She turned left and pumped her legs as hard as she could. She was always a speedy runner, her longs legs helping with that, and she was never more grateful for that than she was right now. The hallway had a slight curve to it in this part of the building. It always creeped her out somewhat, reminding her of the subway scene in *American Werewolf in London.*

Great thing to think about right now, she thought.

Instead of a werewolf chasing you, you have a psychotic Santa Claus.

She glanced behind her once again, not breaking stride. Still no followers. She forged ahead, handling the curve without slowing down a bit.

She came to end of the hallway. Just ahead was the stairwell. One flight of stairs, and the lab would be right there.

Thank god, Samantha thought, slightly out of breath. She raced into the stairwell and bounded the steps three at a time. She emerged back into second floor hallway, and there was the lab, just as she knew it would be. She pulled her badge from the pocket of her scrubs, almost dropping it but snagging the lanyard that it was hooked to. She held it up to the access contraption. At first nothing happened, and a surge of panic shot through her. But after shaking it for a few seconds, the contraption beeped, the little light above turned green, and Samantha yanked the door open. She jumped inside, the door closing behind her. She heard the sound of the door clicking in place, locking automatically.

Samantha felt a momentary sense of relief having achieved her goal of reaching the safety of the lab. But doubts quickly invaded her positivity.

Now you're trapped in here, she thought. No other way out of the lab. If he finds you in here, you're stuck.

Yeah, but he can't get in. And the impenetrable glass should keep you safe.

Yeah, it should. *But is it really bullet proof? Or are the "higher ups" full of shit?*

Well, it may get to be tested real soon.

Maybe he won't even find me in here, she hoped. He didn't seem to be in much of a rush to follow me. Maybe he took a wrong turn and is going to end up in a totally different part of the hospital. Hell, maybe he thought better of his plan, and decided to call it a night and go home.

Fat chance of that.

Anyone who's spent apparently a lot of time stalking you and mapping this whole thing out probably won't decide to change his mind all of a sudden.

Okay, calm down, she told herself. Stop guessing what *might* be happening and deal with the here and now and what you *do* know. You're safe for the time being, but it's probably not the best idea to stand right in front of the glass door in case he was able to follow you. Hell, maybe your phone will even work in here, and you can call for some damn help.

She was about to turn around to look for a place to hunker down when someone grabbed her shoulder.

12

OH, IT'S YOU

Samantha spun around, knocking the arm away from her. She raised her arms, fists at the ready.

"Whoa there," Randy said, taking a step back from Samantha, his palms up in the universal peace position. "It's just me."

It took a moment for Samantha to realize that she wasn't in any immediate danger, that it wasn't Jared who magically found a way into the lab. She unclenched her fists, lowered her arms, and exhaled.

"What's going on," Randy asked, also looking more relaxed now that it didn't appear he was going to get pummeled by Samantha. "You don't usually come in here, and you looked like you were ready to beat the shit out of me."

Samantha wouldn't exactly consider herself friends with Randy, but they got along with each other during work hours, and they even had lunch together a few times when coincidentally taking breaks at the same time. He always seemed cheerful, and that was something Samantha appreciated in the ever stressful environment that they both worked in.

"We need to get away from the door," Samantha said, ignoring Randy's question. She looked past him, searching for a good place to stay out of sight from Jared.

"Why? What's going on?" Randy was starting to sound a little more nervous himself.

Samantha ignored him and walked further into the lab, continuing to survey her surroundings.

"Hey now," Randy said, a little less patiently. "I'm willing to overlook the fact that you didn't sign in when you came into the lab, because we're cool like that. And I'm also willing to forgive you for being ready to punch me in the face. But you're starting to make me kind of nervous here. What exactly is the matter?"

Samantha realized he was right. She turned around and faced Randy. "Sorry I busted in here without much explanation, but we have an emergency. I can't believe I'm saying this, but there's a crazy guy out there dressed like Santa Claus. He killed Wanda." She left out the part about him being someone she had dated.

Randy flashed a crooked smile, his first instinct assuming that she must be joking. It wasn't a very funny joke, but she couldn't be serious. Could she?

But he quickly accepted that she was not joking. Her demeanor said it all.

"Holy shit, you're serious, aren't you?"

"Unfortunately, yes," Samantha said, resuming her search for a good place to hide. "I took off from the scene pretty fast, but I can't be sure he didn't follow me."

"Well I appreciate you attempting to bring him in here with *me*."

"Yeah, well, sorry about that."

"Okay, well let's think here. Have you tried to call for help yet?"

"Yeah, when I heard the gunshots. No signal, as usual."

"Gunshots?"

"Yeah, gunshots. I told you, he killed Wanda."

"Well for some reason, I pictured him strangling her to death. I guess that's not the way they kill people these days."

"Oh yeah, I guess I also forgot to mention that he killed the security guard and the skinny white girl."

"Shit."

"Yeah. Not good."

They stood in silence for a few seconds, each lost in their own thoughts of what to do next.

"Well," Randy said, breaking the silence. "You said you're not sure he followed you, right? Maybe he won't come back this way."

"That's what I'm hoping," Samantha replied. "But now I'm thinking about the other people in the hospital. I know it's pretty empty tonight, but still. Even if he doesn't come back here to kill us, there are others, some of them incapacitated patients, ripe for the killing."

Samantha and Randy looked at each other, neither sure what to say or do. Randy broke the silence.

"Okay, why don't you try to call for help again," he said, rummaging through his pocket. "Here, try my phone, too." He plucked the phone out of his scrub pants and tossed it to Samantha.

"What are you going to do," she asked as she made a nice catch from the low throw.

"I'm going to see if I can figure out what's going on out there."

"I just told you what's going on out there," Samantha whisper shouted. "Jared's out there with a fucking gun and he killed three people already. You want to be the fourth?"

"Jared? You know this guy?"

Shit.

"Don't worry about it," Samantha tried to dismiss the slip.

"Well, shit, that could be useful information," Jared persisted. "How do you know this guy? Is he some psycho boyfriend from your past?"

Knowing he wasn't going to let it go, Samantha replied to Randy. "Okay, yes, it's a guy I dated for a little bit. I have no idea why he's here or why he's killing people."

Randy smirked. "Shit, what did you do to this guy?"

"Ha ha," Samantha said. "Very funny. Now if you're done being a wise ass, try to remember that he already killed three people and he has a gun. We have to figure out what we're going to do."

"Right," Randy acknowledged. "Go ahead and see if either of our phones work. I'll take a quick look out there."

"What part of 'he has a gun' don't you seem to understand?" Samantha said, becoming increasingly annoyed with Randy's cavalier attitude towards the situation. "Don't go out there."

"I'm just going to take a quick listen. You can't hear a damn thing in this lab, and I want to see if I can hear anything. We can't stay in here forever."

Jesus Christ, Samantha thought, knowing he wasn't going to listen to her. "Fine, take your damn listen and get the hell back in here. Hopefully the bigwigs were right about the unbreakable glass in this place and we'll at least be safe in here for the time being."

"Righto," Randy said, winking and giving her the thumbs up. He walked over to the lab entrance, swiped the badge that was around his neck, and opened the door. Samantha fiddled with her phone, then Randy's, glancing between the phones and Randy's ill advised investigation. Neither phone was getting a connection.

"No luck," she said. She looked up to see Randy now standing in the hallway.

"What the fuck are you doing," she said. "Get the hell back in here."

Randy strolled back into the lab, stopping in the doorway. "Just trying to see if I can hear anything. It's dead quiet out there."

"Okay, well get the hell back in here and close the goddamn door."

"Alright, alright," coming fully into the lab. He stuck his head out into the hallway for one more listen.

Jesus Christ, what's the matter with this guy, Samantha thought. Does he have a death wish or something?

As if to answer her question, a gunshot blast sounded through the lab, causing Samantha to drop both of the phones and jump back a step. Randy crumpled to the floor, a splash of red now coating the glass door where his head had been just seconds before.

Samantha hustled over to Randy. He lay motionless, a hole in his head and a pool of blood quickly expanding underneath him. His dead body lay in the lab entranceway, forcing the door to remain open.

Samantha didn't bother to look into the hallway. Aside from not wanting the get shot herself, she already knew that Jared was out there. Either that or another gunman was patrolling the hospital. Either way, the urgent task at hand was getting Randy out of the way so she could close the door.

She grabbed his ankles and started tugging. At first, he glided easily across the floor. The door slowly started to close as less and less of Randy's body blocked it. But just as his head was the last hurtle that needed to be cleared, he got stuck.

Samantha yanked, but Randy's body kept springing back to where it seemed to want to go. She pulled with all of her strength, but some part of his head was holding fast to the edge of the door.

Samantha hopped over to the jam, grabbed his head by his blood soaked hair, and pulled up. The head moved a few inches, but wouldn't budge past that. She looked closer to determine what exactly was getting caught, but it was difficult to tell with all of the blood and brain matter in the area. She couldn't be sure, but it looked like the corner of the door was wedged into the side of his head. Probably where the bullet had made the hole.

Jesus Christ, how is that even possible?

She reached down to dislodge whatever was keeping Randy's head stuck. She held the door open with one hand, and slid her other hand down the side of the bloody head. She tried to pull the head away from the door, with no luck.

Yep, it's stuck alright.

She slid her hand down further into the pulp, trying to separate it from the door. She could feel that the door was indeed now inserted into Randy's cranium. She continued pushing her hand down into his pulverized skull, using her fingers to work it away from the door. Her fingers finally made it all the way through the slop and to the floor, and she thought that she may have just made the separation big enough to allow the door to close. And the door did indeed move in further a few inches, but caught once again.

"Jesus fucking Christ," Samantha mumbled through clenched teeth. She dared not look, but she could practically feel Jared's leering face smiling down on her, his hot breath brushing against the back of her neck.

She reached both hands into Randy's open skull, got a good handhold, and yanked. She yanked a second time, harder. She apologized internally to Randy, but she needed to get him the hell out of the damn doorway. She continued yanking, grunting with each pull, and beginning to move the head more with each jerk. Finally, putting maximum effort into one last tug, she ripped a large chunk of Randy's skull away from his body. She fell backwards into the lab, the skull fragment falling into her lap. The remaining part of Randy's head was apparently no longer enough to make a suitable doorstop, as the door started to close.

Samantha sighed with relief.

But the positive feeling didn't last long.

The door was just about to close completely, locking her safely inside, when two fingers slipped in between the door and the latch. The door was propelled open. And over Randy's corpse now stood Jared.

"Merry Christmas, babe."

AND YOU THOUGHT THIS CHRISTMAS WOULD BE BORING

Another gunshot rang through the hospital, and Zack again almost fell from the start it gave him. It had been quiet for a few minutes, and he was starting to convince himself he had imagined the previous noises. But there was no doubt about this one.

And it sounded closer.

But who could really tell, he thought. Who knows how sounds echo in this place? You might think the gunshot was coming from just up ahead, around that corner, when really it's right behind you...

He turned and looked over his should, his heart now beating a mile a minute.

Nothing there.

Of course not, he thought. It came from up ahead.

Didn't it?

Zack was now on the second floor, and his plan had been to slowly make his way to the first floor entrance. That was where he had guessed the initial gunshots had come from. But although he wanted to investigate and potentially even help if able, he was honestly not in a huge rush to get to the scene of the crime.

But now it sounded like the last shot had come from the floor he was now on. Zack wasn't sure what to think. The only thing he knew for certain was that he heard multiple loud noises, and he was pretty positive they came from a gun being fired. And being in a hospital, that probably wasn't a sound you wanted to hear (not that you really wanted to hear it in any public places). Other than that, he couldn't be positive of anything.

With no better ideas, he took a deep breath, let it out, and moved ahead.

He came to a turn in the hallway. The only options now available were to turn left or go back.

The gunman could be right around the corner, he thought. You round the bend and bang, bullet to the brain. Game over for Zack.

Not likely, he decided. Why would he be waiting just for you, ready to shoot as soon as you turn the corner?

Who knows? Why do mass shooters do anything they do? Trying to figure out the inner thoughts of a gun toting psycho probably isn't the best course of action for surviving the night.

What the hell, Zack decided. You've come this far. You don't know where the sounds came from, or even where you are in the building at this point. Might as well take a peak.

Probably nothing there anyway. This isn't a movie, where scary things lurk around every corner.

Hell, maybe it wasn't even gunshots you heard. Maybe it was some weird hospital equipment going kaput, and you'll turn the corner to see the repairmen making everything better.

He inched his way to the edge of the wall, took a deep breath, and leaned forward. Any slim hopes he had of his fairy tale scenario being true were quickly abated.

Zack wasn't exactly sure what he was looking at at first glance, but he knew instinctively it wasn't good. About twenty yards from where he peaked around the corner, stood a massive guy in a Santa Claus suit. He couldn't see the man's face, as it looked like he was holding open a door and peering into a room. And he was standing over a body. And a pool of blood, seemingly coming from the body he stood over.

Zack abruptly pulled his head back out of sight. He leaned against the wall, unbelieving of what he just witnessed.

What do I do now?

14

HERE'S YOUR PRESENT, BASTARD!

Jared stepped over Randy's corpse and fully entered the lab. Still on the floor, Samantha crab walked away from him. The door closed behind them.

"Good god," Samantha said. "What are you doing, Jared?"

Jared smirked. "Yeah, I admit the plan didn't quite go, well, according to plan." He chuckled at his lame joke. "And maybe this Santa suit was a bit much," he continued, looking at his blood stained attire. "Sure as hell didn't help me get in here without a fuss, like I figured it would."

Samantha stared at him, trying to remember if there was any sign of this insanity when they dated a few months back.

"But hey," Jared continued. "I made it in, and here we are. Together, just like we were meant to be."

Yeah, it's a regular Hallmark Christmas movie.

Jared bent down and reached out for Samantha. She flinched, instinctively trying to back up away from his touch. But she didn't move more than a few inches before her back bumped into one of the counters placed in the lab. Jared's hand found hers, and he slipped it in delicately. He then pulled his arm upward, helping Samantha off of the ground.

"I understand you're a little surprised to see me," Jared said, perhaps noticing the shocked look on Samantha's face. "It was meant to be somewhat of a surprise, but not quite this much of a ruckus. But oh well."

Yeah, 'oh well.' Just a few dead people at the hands of a deranged Santa Claus. After all, you can't make an omelet without breaking a few eggs.

Good grief, I need to get out of here, Samantha thought. But how?

No sense trying to talk sense into him, Samantha knew. He obviously wasn't going to suddenly see the error of his ways, and even if some part of his brain did, it probably wouldn't end well for either of them.

Have to play to his desires. Which apparently center around me.

"Look, Jared," Samantha said, doing her best to remain calm. She thought her voice quivered, but hoped he couldn't tell. "I appreciate all of your efforts here." Jared smiled, looking very pleased with himself. "But to be honest, you made kind of a mess here." She tried to let out a little laugh, as if to say she wasn't *really* bothered by everything he had done. Jared's smile faded ever so slightly.

"I think," Samantha went on, "that it might be for the best if you left the hospital for now."

Jared's smile evaporated.

"Just for now," Samantha piped in quickly. "I'm afraid someone else might have heard the shots and called the police."

"Oh, I agree," Jared chimed in. "We definitely do need to get going. Let me take you away on my magical sleigh. The reindeer are ready to go."

Oh man, is he out to lunch.

"That would be great," Samantha lied, "but I think that would be too suspicious if we both left right now." She wasn't sure what that even meant, but the words were now just flowing out of her. "You go now, and I can meet up with you later." As soon as the words came out of her mouth, she knew they were obvious lies, but she hoped that Jared was so far gone that he wouldn't notice.

Jared squinted his eyes, and his smile transformed into a grimace.

Apparently not as far gone as you hoped.

Before she had to time to even think about talking her way out of her predicament, Jared's left arm shout out, and he backhanded her across the face. The force of the blow knocked her to the floor.

"You ungrateful bitch," he spat down at her. "Can't you see everything I've done for you tonight? First of all, it's very rude that you don't appreciate it. And second, you think your obvious lies are going to trick me. What do you think I am, an idiot?"

Samantha put her hand against her stricken cheek. She wasn't confident that her attempt to trick him would work, but she hadn't expected him to snap so quickly, either.

This isn't going to end well.

And just like that, Jared's expression changed once again. The rage was gone, and he instead simply looked sad.

"I'm sorry, Honey," he said lovingly. "I didn't mean to do that, but you really need to learn to be more appreciative. Here, let me help you up." He reached out a hand, but Samantha did not respond this time. She began to crawl backwards once more, the lab table now to her side."

Jared sighed and began to rub his temples. "Okay, I can see that you're just not ready for this. But that's okay. We have the rest of our lives for me to show you that we were meant to be together."

Samantha scrambled to her feet and ran around to the other side of the lab table.

"Why are you making this difficult?" Jared asked.

Trying to trick him had only gotten her slapped in the face, so she decided to try a different tact. "Jared, why are you doing this?"

Jared sighed again, his frustration clearly growing. "Because I love you," he said, as though it was obvious.

"But Jared, we only went out a few times."

"Yes, it was the greatest time of my life. And it's clear that we are meant to be together. I don't understand why you don't see that."

Okay, the honesty approach isn't going to work any better, Samantha could clearly see. *But you're running out of options. There's only one way out of the lab, and he's blocking the exit.*

"Look, we can do this the easy way or the hard way," Jared said. "But either way, you're coming with me."

Samantha looked around the lab, desperately searching for a way out of this mess. The lab wasn't small, but it was filled with tables, desks, and all kind of lab equipment. There wasn't much room to run. She was quick, but even if she could outrun Jared, the current location didn't allow for much free movement.

"Okay, that does it," Jared said. With no warning, he lunged across the table like a giant cobra, smashing beakers and vials with his body, and spilling unidentified substances. The attack was so sudden that Samantha had no time to react, and Jared was able to grab the front of her scrubs in his meaty fist. He then dragged her across the table towards him.

"I'm sorry to be so rough with you," he said, "but like you said, we might not have much time left before someone else tries to interfere. And you didn't really leave me much choice." He continued to drag her by her scrubs top, knocking over lab equipment as her torso slid across the table and towards him. Her arms flailed, desperately trying to grab onto something to stop him from pulling her closer. But there was nothing to grab. Nothing that was fastened to the table, anyway.

Samantha was tugged across the length of the table, finally falling over the other side. She thumped on the floor, Jared still clutching the fabric of her scrubs. "Here, let me help you up so we can --," he started to say, but never got the chance to finish. Samantha propelled her arm forward, emptying the contents of the only thing she was able to grab while being dragged across the table.

Jared started screaming as soon as the liquid hit his face. Along with the screaming, Samantha could hear sizzling noises. Sounds like bacon frying, she thought. But the smell didn't match that mental image. Instead, the aroma of burning flesh invaded her nostrils.

Must have been some type of acid, Samantha decided.

What the hell kind of hospital leaves acid laying around unprotected, she wondered.

Who cares? In this case, the hospital's crappy standards may have just saved your life!

By this point, Jared's screaming had subsided, and he had his hands covering his face. Samantha could see smoke coming out from between his fingers.

Holy shit, what kind of acid was that?

Jared slowly moved his hands away. Gooey strands connected his hands to his face, stretching as he lowered his arms. They appeared to be melted skin. A myriad of large blisters covered his burnt face, some of them popping as she looked at him. Blood spurted out of them as the mini explosions occurred, mixing with the blood already present on his face. The entirety of Jared's face was either melting or popping off of him.

"What the fuck did you do to me?" he shouted, blood and spittle spraying from his now deformed lips.

Jesus Christ, what *did* you do to him, Samantha wondered. She was rooted to the spot, disgusted by what she was seeing, but unable to turn away. She only snapped out of it once it was too late, and Jared grabbed her with both hands. He picked her up with ease and threw her away from him. Her body became airborne, and her back smashed into the far wall, crashing into shelves of lab equipment. Glass shattered and fell all around her.

"I can see that I made a mistake," Jared whimpered through his pain, the sizzling noises beginning to fade. "You obviously don't give a shit about anyone but yourself." He reached down to the waistband of his baggy red pants and put his hand around the firearm that he had lifted from the security guard. He pulled it free and aimed it at Samantha, who now sat on the floor, surrounded by broken glass and collapsed shelves.

"But if you're not willing to be with me here on Earth, I'll have to settle for us being together forever in the afterlife."

Samantha knew there was nothing she could say to stop Jared from the crazy path he was on. She was going to die tonight. Her life was about to be over at the age of twenty-nine. She closed her eyes and waited for the end to come, hoping that it would at least be quick.

But when the howls of pain permeated the lab, she opened her eyes.

15

AND ANOTHER!

Jared stood still, seemingly frozen in place. The gun dropped from his hand, clattering to the floor, and giving Samantha another jump.

What the hell just happened, Samantha wondered.

Jared began to convulse. It started out with barely perceptible body tremors, but the intensity quickly increased. Foam began to seep out of his now mutilated mouth, mixing with his blood and gooey skin, creating a disgusting frothy substance. It started to pour out of him faster, covering his chin and the front of his outfit.

As the foaming at the mouth lessened, Jared's shaking became more violent. His body performed as though it was being controlled by a puppeteer on speed. The shaking intensified rapidly, and for a second, Samantha thought his whole body might simply explode. But just as quickly as it had started, it came to a halt. Jared's body went limp, and he crumpled to the floor in a heap.

And there stood Zack.

Samantha did a double take. *Is that the kid from the fifth floor?*

He looks about as confused as I am, Samantha thought. What the hell just happened?

The two looked at each other in silence for a moment, both taken aback by what had just transpired.

"Hi," Zack said, breaking the silence.

"Hi yourself," Samantha reciprocated. "What are you doing here?" she asked.

Zack looked slightly embarrassed at the question. "Well, I was, uh, bored in my room, so I came down here to get a snack. And then I heard the gunshots and came to investigate." Zack still wasn't sure if he was trying to hide from the potential danger or help out, but he didn't need to let Samantha know that.

"And then I came this way," Zack continued, beginning to talk faster, "and I saw a huge guy wearing a Santa suit and a dead body, and I didn't know what to do, but I ended up going over to see what was going on and next thing I knew I was in here and I saw him attacking you so I grabbed the two needles and stuck them in his back." Zack took a deep breath after getting out his story.

Samantha looked back down at Jared's body. She hadn't noticed initially, but sure enough, there were two quite intimidating looking syringes sticking up from Jared's back. And it appeared that they hadn't just been jammed into him, but the plungers had both been depressed completely. If anything had been in those syringes, it was now inside Jared.

Zack looked down at the syringes as well. "I'm sorry," he said, talking more calmly now. "I didn't mean to kill him. I just didn't know what to do. He looked like he was going to kill you, and the needles were there, and I just grabbed them and…"

Samantha held up her hand in an attempt to reassure him. "Nothing to be sorry about," she said. "I'm not sure what just happened to him, but if you hadn't done what you did, I would probably be dead right now. So thank you."

Zack blushed and gave a nervous smile.

"Who knows," she continued. "He might not even *be* dead."

Zack's smile vanished.

"We should really get out of here and get some help," Samantha said, pushing herself off of the floor. "Whether he's dead or not, we need to call the police." She put her hand on her lower back and grimaced. The impact with the wall hadn't done her any favors, but she thought she'd be okay.

Zack hopped over Jared's prone body and reached out to help Samantha the rest of the way up. She clutched his hand and got to full standing position.

"Thanks," she said, brushing herself off.

"You okay?" Zack asked, seeming to have calmed down since his arrival at the lab.

"Yeah, I'll be fine," Samantha said. "Getting thrown across the room by a muscle bound Santa Claus isn't going to slow me down."

"Wait a minute," she said, looking up at Zack. "How did you even get in here? This door is supposed to be secure, only able to be opened with a badge." She held up her badge to show him.

"I don't know, I just walked in."

Enough of Randy's brains probably got in between the door and the frame to keep the door from latching completely, Samantha thought.

Well, your head allowed Jared to come in here, Randy, but your brains also helped to let in my savior. She felt bad for the thought as she looked down at Randy's mutilated corpse. Randy was a good guy and deserved much better than this.

"Okay, well let's get the hell out of here and call the police. This damn hospital is full of dead zones, so we'll have to find a landline phone to guarantee we can call out."

Jared's body was blocking their most direct route towards the lab exit. Zack had hopped over him when going to help Samantha, but she had no desire to follow the same path. She'd seen enough horror movies to know that you never walked near the body of the bad guy, or you were just asking for trouble.

"Let's take the long way around, if you don't mind," she said to Zack. She took his hand and was just about to lead them on their circuitous route out of the lab when Zack spoke.

"Uh, Samantha?"

She looked back at Zack. "Yes?"

"I think he's moving."

16

SANTA, WHAT BIG MUSCLES YOU HAVE

They both stared at Jared as Zack's words were proven to be correct. Jared was indeed moving.

Or at least, part of him was moving.

He wasn't moving in the normal way a person would when waking up, or getting up off of the floor. He seemed to still be unconscious, dead, or whatever he in fact was. But there was clear movement coming from under his clothes.

"Um, is it just me, or does something look weird with the way he's moving," Zack said, not letting go of Samantha's hand.

"No, it's not you," Samantha replied, staring at Jared's body.

"We should really get out of here."

"Hold on just one second."

What the hell, Zack thought. Why are we not getting out of here as fast as possible?

The strange movement continued under Jared's clothing.

"I don't mean to be difficult," Zack said, "but I really think we should get going. That psycho is either alive or something else weird is happening. Either way, I really don't want to be around to find out what it is."

"You can go," Samantha said, still gazing at Jared's body. "Between the acid and whatever you stabbed him with, I assumed he was dead. But if he's still alive and needs medical help, I can't just leave him here. Psycho or not."

"He just tried to kill you," Zack said, louder than he meant to.

Samantha pulled her gaze from Jared and turned towards Zack. "Look, you can leave if you want. In fact, it's probably a good idea. Go and get some help. But I'm staying until I know what's going on. And yes, he tried to kill me, but he doesn't look like much of a threat right now. And it's also not my job to determine who gets medical treatment and who doesn't." She let go of Zack's hand.

Dammit.

Samantha turned her attention back to Jared, and they stood in silence for a few seconds.

"You're right," Zack said, not actually believing his own words. But her hand had felt so good, and he felt compelled to stay with her. She might be slightly pissed at him, but if he split now, he knew any chance he ever had of seeing her after this night would be reduced to nil. "I'll stay with you."

They both looked at Jared. The movement had seemed to spread across his whole body now. It was like little waves rippling underneath his clothes. But the waves started to grow. And the Santa suit started to expand, stretching taut across Jared's body.

And then the suit began to burst at the seams.

"Zack?"

"Yes?"

"I think I changed my mind. Let's get out of here."

"Good idea."

Samantha and Zack only managed two steps before Jared let out a skull shattering scream. They both stopped in their tracks, letting out yelps of surprise themselves.

And then things really got crazy.

Everything happened so fast. As Jared began to writhe around on the floor, his clothing bulged and burst apart along his entire body. And as the clothes tore away in places, Zack and Samantha could see Jared's actual body growing. His already large muscles were growing enormous. But it wasn't just his muscles that were growing. His entire frame was increasing in size.

Jared pushed himself up onto his knees. He staggered to a standing position. His Santa suit was a tattered mess, and he threw off the remains of his red coat. The pants were splitting in places, but managed to stay on his body. The little red Santa hat remained atop his now huge cranium.

If it hadn't been so terrifying, it would have been comical.

Jared roared once again, his body continuing to ripple and grow. His skin itself was moving, as if the muscles and tendons underneath were doing a macabre dance. The ripples subsided as his skin appeared to become tighter, much like his clothing had done moments earlier.

And just like his clothing, his skin began to burst open.

Bloody mountains of muscle grew out of the newly formed crevices. Loose skin flapped at the sides of his protruding muscles, most notably in his arms and chest. His legs did not appear to be growing to the same degree as his upper body, so although his pants stretched ever tighter, they somehow managed to remain on his lower half despite the growing tears in the red fabric.

The entire transformation took place in less than thirty seconds. Jared, or what used to be Jared, held out his gorilla-like arms and looked down at himself, seemingly taking in what he had become. Zack and Samantha took in the entire show, completely slack jawed.

"Holy shit, it's a fucking Santa Beast," Zack spurted out.

The Santa Beast, finished with examining his new body, looked up at its two enemies.

It smiled. Its tongue slithered out to lick its bloody lips.

"Oh shit," Zack and Samantha said in unison.

The beast looked up and bellowed to the heavens as it beat its chest with its fists.

17

RUN!

"Let's get the fuck out of here!"

While the Santa Beast was carrying on and not paying close attention to his potential victims, Samantha and Zack ran around the lab table. They needed to evacuate the lab, and they sure as hell weren't going to run directly past the monstrosity that stood before them. Samantha thought for sure he would stop his frenzied cries as soon as they made for their escape, but he still did not seem to notice them. They scooted behind the creature and Samantha pulled on the lab door handle, half expecting it to be stuck. But it opened with ease, Randy's blood and brains apparently keeping it nice and oiled up. They skipped over Randy's corpse and ran into the hallway.

Samantha couldn't believe they made it out of there alive.

Don't get too cocky, she told herself. There's a fucking seven foot tall Santa Claus monster back there. Who knows what he's capable of?

Or what else may happen tonight. Apparently, anything is possible.
What a Christmas!

"This way," Samantha said, turning left and sprinting ahead.

Zack ran after her. "Where are we going?"

"The hell out of here. The stairs are just ahead. We'll take those down to the first floor and run like hell to the exit."

"Sounds good to me."

Samantha and Zack ran down the hallway, although it wasn't a long trip to the stairwell. Luckily, the lab was located at the far end of the hall, which was in close proximity to the stairs.

They reached the door to the stairwell, and Samantha pushed it open, not breaking stride. She ran in but abruptly stopped. Zack bumped into her.

"Fuck," she shouted out of frustration. In front of her were multiple hospital carts jammed between the railings of the stairs, blocking their escape. Samantha figured that they would be able to move them, but it would probably take a few minutes at minimum, and by then, Jared would be upon them and ripping their heads off.

Not Jared, Samantha thought. Whatever that thing is, it's not Jared anymore.

It's a goddam monster.

Or like Zack said, a fucking Santa Beast.

Whatever it is, it's not going to get us that easily.

"Okay, we're going up," she said to Zack.

"Up?" Zack questioned. "Isn't there another way down? Going up doesn't seem like the best idea."

"The elevator's on the other side of the hospital. I'm not risking running past the lab again and having that thing snag us. We can go up and circle back around."

Not wanting to run past the monster himself, Zack didn't argue with the plan. He nodded, and the pair ran up the stairs, Samantha taking three steps at a time to his two.

Damn, she's in good shape, Zack thought. Despite everything they were going through at the moment, he couldn't help but notice the way Samantha's pants hugged her perfectly shaped behind as she extended her legs up the stairs.

Okay, well you're probably going to die tonight, but at least you got a nice view while fleeing for your life.

"I know we're running away from a murdering monster, but could you maybe slow down just a tiny bit," Zack said between breaths. "I did just have surgery, you know."

"Sorry," Samantha responded. She slowed down, although Zack still had trouble keeping up.

"Let's go up to the fifth floor and get out there," she said down to Zack, who was doing his best to keep up. "I don't relish the idea of going up, but I do like the idea of a couple of floors separating us from him." She raced past the doors that led to the third and fourth floors, and bounded up the next flight of stairs.

Upon arriving on the fifth floor landing, she pushed the handle bars to open the door that would lead them into the hallway. She held the door for Zack, who made his way up behind her.

"Thanks," Zack said as walked through the doorway, entering the fifth floor.

Samantha followed, letting the door close gently in order to avoid any extra noise that could lead the Santa Beast to them.

"Let's duck into one of the rooms up here for a second. I want to try and call for help again. Sometimes you can get a better signal on the upper floors." Zack followed her lead.

"So," Zack said as he walked slightly behind Samantha, "do you know that guy?"

"Why do you ask that?" Samantha replied as she focused on a good place to hunker down for a few minutes.

"Well, it all happened pretty fast, but before I stabbed him with the needles, I thought I heard the two of you talking like you knew each other."

Samantha sighed, deciding she didn't care anymore if her secret was out. "Yes, not one of my proudest decisions in life, but I dated him a while back. Apparently, he wants to resume the relationship. But I can say with confidence that it's not going to happen."

"Oh, man," Zack said. "You went out with that thing?"

Samantha rolled her eyes. "I just said it wasn't one of my proudest moments. And we only went out a few times. I had no idea he was obsessed with me, and I honestly don't know why."

"That's easy," Zack said. "You're super hot."

Samantha blushed. *Oh, the men in my life.*

"Okay, let's get down to business," she said, trying to change the subject. She found a room that was unoccupied and seemed as good as any other place to hide out for a moment and figure out their next plan of action. "Let's go in here and get out of the direct line of sight." She entered the room and Zack followed without argument. She peeked out into the hallway one last time, and upon seeing no one present, neither man or monster, she closed the door.

18

THE GREATEST CHRISTMAS PRESENT EVER

Ending his Neanderthal-like ritual, the Santa Beast stood in the lab marveling at what he had become. His body was now bursting with raw energy. No longer encumbered by human thoughts and emotions, he felt driven by pure animalistic instincts.

Hunt. Kill. Fuck.

And all of his senses had elevated, allowing for these base instincts to reach their fullest potential. He no longer felt the need to think and plan things out. Deciding the best course of action was no longer necessary. No, his body could now respond to his impulses, following his natural instincts.

And his body had also physically changed to meet his newfound needs. He had already been a large man who was in excellent shape. Hours each day in the gym had made sure of that. But now he was so much more. He could feel the power pulsing through him. As if to explore his newly increased strength, he reached out and grabbed the lab table by the corner and easily flipped it over onto its side. The table slid across the floor, the remaining items on the counter top clattering to and shattering on the floor.

The inhuman Santa Claus smiled, his acid scarred face a terrifying sight to behold had there been anyone there to witness it.

And there was something else. Something in the clouded muddle of his brain that was calling out to be recognized. Something to be the target of these risen, animalistic needs.

Samantha.

The name itself was only a passing memory at this point, just a fleeting titch of a thought that scratched at the corners of his mind. But the person itself was not forgotten. The creature had an aching need for her. He needed to have her. For her to be his in every way.

Every single way.

He lumbered towards the door, pushed it open, and left the lab.

19

HIDING FROM A PSYCHOPATHIC MONSTER, BUT IT COULD BE WORSE...

"**S**till no fucking signal," Samantha growled at her phone. She had remained remarkably calm during their ordeal, but Zack could tell that it was starting to get to her.

Not that he could blame her.

And he knew he didn't help anything with his idiotic comments.

She probably feels bad enough about the whole thing, Zack thought, without you making a big deal of her going out with him.

But it was surprising, he told himself. You couldn't help but be a little surprised, right?

Yeah, well you didn't make things any better by calling her hot. Real good time to try to pick her up, or whatever the hell you were doing.

Wait, he remembered. Not just hot.

Super hot.

Oh god, he thought. Did you really say that to her?

I couldn't help it. She is fucking hot! And yes, super hot!

"It'll be okay," Zack said, trying to sound reassuring. "We'll figure a way out of this."

Samantha stared at her phone, not saying a word or looking at Zack. She looked extremely tense.

"I'm thinking we should get moving again," Zack said quietly. "We can call for help once we get out of here."

Samantha sighed. "That's the problem. If we get out of here, it may be too late for help."

"What do you mean?"

"Sorry, not trying to be an idiot or talk in riddles. But I'll be honest. I'm very conflicted. My first instinct is to make a run for it and try to get the hell out of here."

"Mine too," Zack blurted out. "Let's go."

"Just hold on a second," Samantha said, holding her palms out in front of her. "Let me think for a minute." She paused, clearly trying to stay calm and take stock of the situation. "I don't mean to be melodramatic, but I am a nurse, and it's my job to help the patients here. Now normally that doesn't include protecting them from crazy Santa Claus monsters, but that's what we're dealing with. I can't just run off and leave them. God knows what he could do to them."

"I don't think we have to worry about that," Zack responded. "He's clearly here for you."

Samantha glared at him. "Thanks."

"Sorry, that didn't come out right." Zack moved over next to her on the hospital bed that she was sitting on. "I just meant that you can't put that much pressure on yourself, trying to save everyone in the hospital. Whatever that thing is, it's trying to kill you. You won't be any good to anybody if you wind up dead."

Samantha looked back down, clearly not convinced.

"And what about me," Zack continued. "I'm a patient, too. Don't you need to take care of me, too?" He had intended to sound funny, doing his best to lighten the mood. But after he said it, he was afraid it sounded like another corny pick up line.

Samantha chuckled. "Yeah, I guess you're right. Sorry, I don't mean to be breaking down like this." She put her head in her hands.

Zack put his hand on her shoulder. "You're hardly breaking down," he said. "You're upset and frustrated about being chased by a monster in a Santa suit. I think that's perfectly understandable. In fact, I'd say you're holding up pretty well."

"Well thanks. Anyway, I was going to say, before I was so rudely interrupted," she said as she flashed a crooked smile at Zack, "that all of that being said, the place is pretty much a ghost town tonight. I honestly don't know that we have any patients staying overnight. Other than you, of course."

"Thanks for remembering me."

"And the staff is pretty limited, too."

"Yeah, and it's *really* limited now."

Samantha ignored the crass comment and picked her head up, rubbing her chin. "I just can't believe this is happening," she said. "I mean, aside from the fact that he's now a monster and all."

Now Zack was the one that chuckled.

"I'm not saying he was the greatest guy in the world or anything," she continued. "But I never thought something like *this* would happen. I mean, sure, he was upset when we stopped going out, or whatever it was we were doing, but I had no idea how hard he took it."

"I guess you had quite the effect on him," Zack said, gently rubbing her shoulder. He tried to sound light.

"We only went out a few times. I don't understand how it came to this."

"Like I said, you had quite an effect on him. I can understand it. I mean, aside from the killing people and stuff."

Samantha looked up and faced Zack. "Thanks," she said, putting her hand on his knee. "You're sweet."

Holy shit, Zack thought. She's beautiful.

And she's touching me! Whoever thought this would be possible at the beginning of the night?

Sure, we're on the run from a hulking Santa monster, but aside from that, things could definitely be worse.

Samantha didn't look away, and Zack was beginning to get lost in her heavenly eyes. Her hand remained on his knee, and without even thinking about it, he was now rubbing her shoulder, moving on to her general back area.

Oh my god, are we going to kiss?

Yeah, but only if you do something. It won't happen by magic.

What, are you fucking James Bond or something? You're in the middle of a life and death situation here. That monster could come crashing in here any second. This isn't the time to be making it with a girl.

But she is so beautiful...

It only took a few seconds for these thoughts to flow through Zack's brain, but it was too long. The moment had passed. Samantha looked back down at her phone. Zack tried and failed to look casual as he took his gaze away from Samantha.

"If only this goddam thing would work," Samantha said, breaking the awkward silence.

"Yeah," Zack answered, although his mind was still back at what didn't happen.

You really blew it.

No, he told himself. You would have really blown it if you actually *did* do something. She doesn't want to kiss you right now. She's being chased by her ex-boyfriend who's become a seven foot Santa Claus monster. Romance with you is probably not on the top of her list right now.

Fuck it, he thought. Focus on staying alive through the night. If you're dead, you definitely won't have a chance with her or anybody else for that matter.

But still...

Samantha and Zack both had their internal thoughts interrupted when they heard a noise from outside their temporary sanctuary. They looked up simultaneously.

Now what?

20

IT'S CHRISTMAS, AND I'M STILL HORNY

Doctor Riley Simpkins was horny.

She'd been getting caught up with some paperwork for the past hour or so. It was her least favorite part of the job, which was why she had so much to catch up on. But with her headphones on and her music playing from her smartphone, it wasn't so bad. She could get lost in the music as she mechanically filled out forms, and the time went fairly quickly.

But as the time passed, and with the music getting her into a good rhythm with her work, her amorous feelings also began to grow.

Good god, woman. Who gets horny doing paperwork?

Apparently you do.

Riley had always had a healthy sex drive, and it showed no signs of slowing down as she got older. She was hardly over the hill, but she was now in her early forties. And she had the sex drive of a high school boy.

Luckily for her, the years had done nothing to hamper her good looks. At forty-two, she could still turn heads. And she didn't hesitate to take advantage of that fact.

Like with Randy.

Damn, she enjoyed fucking him. She never let on to that of course. Not fully, anyway. Sure, throw him a crumb here and there, but not too much. Randy was a nice guy, the type of guy that always wanted to please people. And he sure as hell had pleased Riley on multiple occasions.

But she couldn't tell *him* that. If he got too comfortable, he would get lazy, the sex would begin to suffer, and she would need to move on to her next conquest. Something that she knew would happen eventually anyway, but she wanted to prolong their physical relationship for a little while longer.

No sense ending a good thing prematurely, she thought, a smile forming on her lips.

It was then that she realized she had unconsciously moved her left hand down under her desk, and she was gently touching herself over her figure hugging skirt while she continued signing papers with her right.

You always have been a good multitasker, she thought.

She closed her eyes and began to rub herself more aggressively. She dropped the pen on her desk, accepting that she wasn't going to get any actual work done for at least the next few minutes. And the way she was feeling right now, probably longer.

She stopped touching herself just long enough to hike her skirt up over her waist. She massaged herself over her panties, but that only lasted for a few seconds before she pushed the fabric aside and began to manipulate herself with no layers of fabric blocking the way. She was already extremely wet, and she plunged both her index and middle finger inside of herself.

"Oh, god," she let out, tilting her head back, the rhythmic movement of her hand intensifying. She pushed her chair back a bit with her feet to give herself some more room to work. She then lifted her right leg, setting her foot on the desktop.

She was really getting lost in the moment now. She had found the rhythm, and she was rapidly bringing herself to an orgasm. She began to run her fingers through her hair with her right hand, unintentionally knocking the headphones off of her head. She barely noticed, and her hand traveled down her neck and landed on her breasts, where she began to massage them and knead her nipples through her blouse. On the verge of ecstasy, she heard the door knock.

At first, she barely heard it, hoped she *didn't* hear it, and continued on with her mission of pleasing herself. But the knock came again, louder this time, and there could be no denying someone was outside of her door. Someone who apparently needed something urgently.

She ceased the touching of her body, noticed the headphones laying on her desk.

Jesus, she thought. If you hadn't knocked them off, you may not have ever heard the knocking at your door. Then you could have finished what you started.

Or, whoever it is out there could have walked in and found you in a somewhat compromising position. She smiled at the thought, feeling almost excited by the possibility of being caught masturbating at her desk.

Maybe it's Randy out there, she thought. Coming back for more.

Her smile grew at the prospect. It better be, she thought. Because if it isn't, whoever is out there may very well get the surprise of their life. After all, I'm horny as hell right now, and I need someone, anyone to finish me off!

The knock came again, although it was more of a pounding this time.

"Alright already," she mumbled to herself. Whoever it was seemed desperate to get in, but Riley assumed it wasn't an actual medical emergency. If it was, she would have been paged over the intercom or called on her phone.

She stood up, straightened her panties, and pulled her skirt down, doing her best to smooth it out. She quickly felt her hair to make sure it wasn't too out of control after her mussing with it. Confident she looked presentable, she walked to the door. She almost stumbled at first, her legs a bit wobbly after her session, but she regained her balance and continued on.

She reached out to grab the door knob, when another pounding came, startling her.

"Good grief," she said, louder this time, and beginning to get annoyed. If that is Randy, he's sounding rather desperate.

Good, she thought. You can have him do whatever you want him to. Not that you can't normally anyway.

She smiled, knowing she was in complete control. She opened the door.

She screamed.

● 21

GUESS WHO

He had been stalking Samantha, driven by instinct and his heightened senses. He was no longer deducing logically where she might have gone. He simply hunted her like any wild animal would do.

But although locked in on Samantha's trail, something intruded.

Another scent. A woman's pheromones were assaulting his senses. And they compelled him to search for their destination.

The Santa Beast lumbered up the stairs, each step creaking under his massive girth. He stopped when he reached the door that led to the third floor.

His new prey was beyond this door.

He pushed on the door, but not recognizing that he needed to press in the metal bar for opening it properly, the door didn't budge. Frustrated, he grunted and kicked the door with his foot. The door gave way with a boom as it splintered into multiple pieces which now littered the hallway. He walked through the threshold, kicking pieces of door out of his way.

His prey was close. He could feel it.

He felt a stirring in his groin which only spurred him on to his destination faster.

Now jogging, his footsteps were audible, had there been anyone around to hear them. So excited was he to locate his prey, he almost ran too far. But he quickly corrected his overzealous mistake and made a quick stop. He took one step back and looked at the door.

In there. His erection grew, straining against the already tight fabric of his pants. He smiled. And a small part of his brain which used to be human told him it was polite to knock before simply barging in.

RILEY'S SCREAM caused both the beast's smile and erection to grow. She backed away, not believing what she found herself staring at.

The beast moved forward, attempting to enter the attractive doctor's office, but his huge bulk prevented him from entering smoothly. He took one cursory glance at the doorway, backed up a step, than catapulted forward. He easily entered the room, knocking pieces of the doorframe off of the wall to allow for his entry.

Dear god, Riley thought. What am I looking at here?

Riley continued to back away from the monster until her rump bumped into her desk.

The Santa Beast advanced on his prey. Riley ran behind the desk, desperately looking for any protection she could find from the monstrous creature standing before her.

The monster's smile only grew. He was enjoying her feeble attempts to escape him.

He had her trapped, and he knew it.

And Riley knew it, too. And this fact only aroused his desires.

The beast lumbered forward, reached the desk, and threw it across the room with ease. It smashed into the wall, the contents of the desk scattering across the floor and parts of the desk itself breaking off.

Nothing stood between Riley and the monster.

Riley screamed again.

And the beast moved in.

Riley put her arms up to block the beast's attack, but it was as about as useful as trying to imprison a rhinoceros with a wall of string. The beast clutched Riley's white blouse with both hands and ripped it open, buttons flying across the room. He smiled at Riley's perfectly formed breasts, now only encumbered by her lacy, turquoise bra.

The beast grabbed her wrists and pinned them against the wall. He smiled as he looked down at his work.

And the smile evaporated as Riley brought her foot up in a quick kick to the beast's groin.

The monstrous brute howled in pain, his erection smashed by the toe of Riley's shoe. He instinctively let go of her wrists as he reached down to cup his wounded genitalia. Riley took the opportunity to run around the moaning monster, racing for the door. She moved as fast as she could, but damn it was hard to run in high heels, and dodging the debris left by the creature's attack surely didn't help anything.

Your outfits are sexy and good for attracting hot lab guys, she thought, but not so hot for evading monsters.

She made it through the destroyed doorway and took two steps into the hallway before a huge claw grabbed her by the back of her collar and yanked her back into the room. The creature spun her around, digging his meaty fists into her shoulders. He snarled at her, drool glistening on his putrid lips and dribbling down his chin.

"Oh shit," Riley breathed as the Santa Beast picked her up and threw her across the room. Her back slammed into the wall, the impact so great that she seemed to almost get indented into the wall for a few seconds before slowly crumpling to the floor. Though dazed, she knew she needed to get up and get the hell out of there. But her body wasn't responding. She needed a few seconds to recover.

A few seconds that she wasn't going to be allowed.

The Santa Beast walked over to her with clear purpose, picked her up, and flung her over his shoulder. He then walked over to the overturned desk, righted it with his one free hand, and tossed Riley down on to the top of it. She let out an "oof" as her belly hit the mahogany wood, knocking the wind out of her.

She gasped for breath, not able to see exactly what the monster was currently doing in her current position. Through her ragged breaths, she tried to turn her head and look behind her, but her head was immediately forced back down into the desk. Her glasses cracked on impact with the desk, causing one of the lenses to shatter, with one of the shards of glass puncturing her eyeball.

Riley screamed out in pain. Behind her, the monster let out a gurgled cackling sound. Seemingly entertained by Riley's agony, he grabbed a handful of her hair in his fist, picked her head up off of the desk, and slammed it down again. Harder this time.

Riley's glasses completely shattered this time, but still hung precariously from her face. A gush of blood shot out from her now shattered nose. And through her pain addled mind, Riley was pretty sure that at least one of her teeth was knocked out of her mouth.

The beast clutched her hair harder, practically ripping it out of her skull. He repeated the violent act a few more times, but as Riley became less conscious and thereby less responsive to his punishments, he was no longer getting the same reaction from his victim that he was enjoying ever so much. Losing interest in that game, he moved on to other endeavors.

Energized by the brutality already inflicted upon his victim, the creature grabbed Riley's skirt and tore it off of her. As he was not in any way attempting to be delicate, and the garment was rather tight, some of Riley's skin came along with it. He tossed the ruined clothing to the floor.

Riley's pink thong was the next thing to go, as the crazed monster easily ripped the lacy fabric with one finger. He pulled his pants down, grabbed Riley hips, and thrust his enormous erection into her.

In his current state, the beast's member was much too large for any normal woman to accommodate, so the entry into Riley was a painful one. She was still in a daze from the beating she had already taken, but the pain that assaulted her from this new attack brought her back to full consciousness. She screamed out once again, bloody spittle spraying from her mouth.

It didn't take long for the brute to get warmed up, and he began pumping harder into Riley. He clutched her more firmly, digging his claws into her tender flesh. His thrusts became more fluid as his enormous erection enlarged Riley's opening and the area was lubricated with her blood.

The pain increasing as he ravaged her body, Riley whimpered on the desk, taking the punishment being dished out to her.

Please god, she thought through the agony. Just let this end already.

And her wish was granted as the festively garbed monster gave one final thrust into her, shooting out what seemed like buckets fool of ejaculate. Riley could actually feel the hot liquid filling up her insides. But there was way too much to be contained in her, and much of it flowed out of her like a faucet that hadn't quite been turned off all the way.

But the monster wasn't completely done with her.

He pulled his empty member out of her. Though it was presumably smaller after he had finished with his assault, the pain was still excruciating for Riley. She moaned in anguish, no longer possessing the strength to give a full out scream. The revolting penis plopped out of Riley with an audible pop, causing one more jolt of pain to course through her ravaged body. The Santa Beast then stood up straight, let out a scream of his own, and began pounding his chest like some kind of deranged jungle creature.

Once done with his ritual, he reached back down and grabbed Riley, flipping her over onto her back. He snipped her bra off with a flashing rake of his hand, exposing her ample breasts. He began to fondle them roughly with his enormous hands, drool forming in the corner of his twisted grin.

Oh god, Riley thought. Why won't this end?

Knowing she couldn't stand another round of being raped by the monstrous maniac, Riley somehow found the inner strength to kick her leg out, connecting squarely with the beast's growing erection.

But she was too weakened from the attack, and the blow had no impact. The Santa Beast barely moved. He stopped groping her for a moment as he looked down at where she had kicked him. No longer smiling, he looked back up at her and growled.

"Oh shit," Riley mumbled through her bloodied lips.

Looking back at the foot that had connected with his groin, the beast wrenched the black shoe off of Riley, fracturing her ankle as he did so. He held it up high over his head, and with the force of a pile driver, he brought it down towards Riley's face. The heel of the shoe embedded itself in her eye socket, blood oozing out around the circumference of the heel.

Riley's body began to twitch. The Santa Beast grabbed her by the waist and rammed his enlarged penis back into her ruined vagina. He thrusted into her with a barbarism seldom witnessed. He continued to rape her savagely long after her body had stopped moving. He finally exploded inside of her once again, letting out a groan of pleasure as he did so.

Mercifully, Riley did not have to suffer through the entire process this time.

She was dead.

It was impossible to say if it was the high heel through her eye socket or the abuse that her body took while being violated in the worst way imaginable. But either way, Riley Johnson's suffering had ended.

The Santa Beast stood up, pulling up his pants as he did so. He looked at the doctor's broken and bloody body laying on the desk. He felt no remorse, or really any emotions at all in viewing what he had done to her. He was a creature that simply followed his instincts now, as sick as they may be. And this unlucky woman was simply a tool that could be used to fill his needs.

But now that he was done with her, another thought worked its way into his mind.

This woman laying here was something he had stumbled upon unintentionally. He had not been seeking her out.

Not like the other one. The one that he was pursuing before this one came along.

Samantha.

The name barely registered with him, but it was still in there, somewhere. Whether he was aware of it or not. But her name didn't matter. He remembered who his prey was. And with this distraction out of the way, he could go back to hunting his true target. He walked to the door and left the doctor's office.

●22

STILL HIDING OUT

"What the fuck was that?" Zack whispered.

"Sounds like someone in the hallway," Samantha whispered back. She stood up and started to move towards the door.

"What the fuck are you doing," Zack said, still whispering, but louder than he intended.

Samantha looked back at Zack, mildly irritated. "I'm going to try to see who's out there."

"It's the fucking Santa Beast!"

Samantha pursed her lips before responding. "It doesn't sound like him," she responded to Zack's panicked reply. "I know it's not huge, but this *is* a hospital. Between the patients and the staff, it's possible there are other people still here."

Zack paused for a moment, feeling a bit silly for his initial panic.

But still, he thought. There is a goddam Santa Claus monster out there...

"Wait a minute," Zack interjected. "I thought you said there weren't hardly any patients or staff here tonight?"

"Okay, you got me there. But if it is Jared, or the Santa Beast or whatever you called him, we can't just hide in here. He'll find us, and then we're really screwed."

"Okay, fine," Zack conceded. "Just be as quiet as possible until we know for sure."

"Oh, good advice. I was planning on stomping around and shouting, but I'll try to be more careful."

Zack held a finger up, preparing to defend his concerns, but decided against it. Samantha clearly wasn't an idiot, and she knew what she was doing. And he had probably already insulted her intelligence with his obvious advice.

You're lowering your chances with her by the second, he thought to himself.

Zack took a deep breath and let it out as quietly as possible. "Okay, I'm sorry," he said. "Just be careful."

Samantha smiled back at Zack, and he felt better. Okay, he thought. I don't think she totally hates you yet. If you make it out of this alive, you may still have a chance.

Yeah, big fucking if.

You might not make it through the next five minutes, depending who or what is out there!

Samantha creeped closer to the door. Zack stood up, steeling himself for what may be coming. He'd found the strength to jump in and help previously tonight, and he hoped he would be able to do so again if warranted. But at the moment, he wasn't feeling very confident in his bravery.

Samantha reached the door and slowly moved her head forward, tilting it to get a better listen as to what may be on the other side. She strained to hear, but no more noises came. She listened for a few more seconds before looking back at Zack. He gave her a look as if to say, "well?" Samantha shrugged her shoulders.

She reached out and grasped the door handle. She slowly began to turn it.

Zack popped up off of the floor. "What are you doing?" he hissed.

Samantha turned her head, glaring at Zack.

Zack pressed his lips together, willing himself to remain quiet.

You may be hot, he thought, but you're going to get us killed with your bravery.

Or stupidity. Not sure which it is.

Oh well, he thought. If you're going to bite the big one, might as well do it in a blaze of glory. At least getting killed by a Santa Claus monster with a beautiful woman by your side wouldn't be a *boring* way to go.

Samantha was back at work on the door handle. She turned it as slowly and quietly as she could. Zack was grateful for her carefulness, but the anticipation was killing him. His heart felt like it was about to leap out of his chest.

Finally, the latch of the door disengaged, making a small clicking sound. But it might as well have sounded like a bomb going off to Zack. He grimaced, half expecting the monster to come smashing down the door after hearing the noise and being alerted to their whereabouts.

But nothing came.

Samantha looked back at Zack once more before slowly opening the door.

Oh Jesus, he thought. Every fiber of his being wanted to run over and stop her from going any further. But he held back.

Samantha pulled the door towards her ever so slowly. Light spilled into the darkened room through the small gap in the doorway. As the opening grew, Zack had more awful visions of monstrous hands shooting into the doorway, ripping the door open the rest of the way.

Samantha continued pulling the door open.

Zack felt as though every one of his muscles was taut. He squinted, bracing for the worst.

The door was open enough to see out of now. Samantha peered around the door, sticking her head out into the hallway ever so slightly.

Oh god, her beautiful head is going to get chopped right off, I know it!

But nothing happened.

Samantha stuck her head out further. She looked left, then right.

Her head did not get chopped off.

Zack let out the breath he had been holding for god knew how long.

Samantha turned back towards Zack. With the light coming in from the hallway, it was difficult to make out her features from inside the darkened room. "Nothing's out there," she said quietly, although no longer feeling the need to whisper.

Thank god, Zack thought, although he still half expected to see a monster pop up from behind Samantha's silhouette.

"I'm thinking we should make a run for it," Samantha said

Zack was afraid she'd say something like that. He didn't totally disagree with her proposal, but leaving the apparent safety of the room they had been hiding out in wasn't super appealing to him. Still, she definitely knew the hospital better than him, so he decided it was best to follow her lead. And being outside the hospital was a glorious thought.

"Lead the way," he said, trying to sound confident in the decision. He began walking over to the doorway when he saw a blur of movement behind Samantha, followed by a yelp from her.

Something grabbed her around the waist.

Samantha spun around, instinctively striking back at her

attacker. Zack ran to the doorway to help, assuming he was ultimately running to his death.

And then he heard another voice. A human voice.

Thank god, Zack thought.

I think.

Zack ran into the hallway, prepared to help Samantha ward off whoever or whatever was attacking her. But upon exiting the room, he was surprised to find Samantha standing next to a man in a long white coat, presumably a doctor.

"You fucking asshole," Samantha said to the newcomer as she gave him a shove to the chest. The doctor grinned, clearly amused by Samantha's reaction.

Zack wasn't sure exactly what was going on here, but he was glad to see it wasn't the Santa Beast that he had to deal with.

That being said, this guy looked like a dick.

He looked youngish, at least for a doctor. Zack guessed mid-thirties, early forties. He was decent looking, but he was too tan and his hair was too gelled up. He clearly thought he was a big shit, and he reminded Zack of the asshole jocks he had to deal with not that long ago in high school.

They're everywhere, he thought. And some of them grow up to join the medical profession.

When the doctor saw Zack emerge from the room, his smile faded. "Who's this guy," he said to Samantha, but stared at Zack.

"This is Zack," Samantha said. "And Zack, this is our resident Dr. Jerkoff."

Dr. Jerkoff chuckled, seemingly pleased with the nickname given to him.

"That name would actually be Dr. Watters," the doctor corrected, extending a hand. Zack shook hands with him and had his hand partially crushed in Watters's overcompensating squeeze. Zack tried to break away after what seemed like an acceptable hand shake period, but Watters held firm. Once Zack gave up, Watters let go.

Jesus Christ, I'm going to need both *arms in a cast!*

"What's going on out here," Zack asked. "For a second, I thought you were being attacked by the monster."

Watters scrunched up his face in an annoying way. "Monster?" he asked.

"No," Samantha jumped in. "Just Dr. Watters here being his usual annoying self."

Zack smiled, appreciating the fact that Samantha wasn't taking any crap from the obviously egotistical doctor.

"Just keeping you on your toes," Watters chimed in. "What are you going to do, report me to the 'me too' people? And what's this about a monster?"

"That doesn't make any sense. And yes, I probably should report you to the 'me too' people, if that was a group that actually existed. You can't just go around grabbing people. You scared me half to death."

"First of all," Watters said, "I don't go around grabbing people. That privilege is just for you. And I hardly *grabbed* you. I'd call it more of a little tickle between friends. And besides, you know you liked it."

This guy really is out to lunch, Zack thought, rolling his eyes.

"I saw that, kid," Watters said to Zack. "You think you're hot shit for hanging out with Sam the hottie here?"

Zack looked at the doctor, not sure how to respond.

"I'm just messing with you," Watters finally said, patting Zack on the shoulder a little too hard. He then leaned in closer to Zack. "But good luck trying to bag her," he said quietly but still loud enough for Samantha to hear. "I've been trying to nail her for years with no luck."

Zack felt relieved at Watters's admission. It seemed clear that

Samantha did not like the cocky doctor, but it was nice to have it confirmed.

Although she *was* with the Santa Beast, he remembered.

Watters stepped back. "Okay, stop trying to distract me. Will someone give me a goddam answer about the monster you so casually mentioned?"

Samantha and Zack looked at each other, not sure how to respond. They both knew the story would sound crazy to anyone hearing it.

"Well?" Watters asked again? "Are you two just going to stare at each other, or are you going to tell me what the hell is going on here?"

Samantha looked back at Watters. "Okay, I'll tell you, but I'm warning you that it's going to sound crazy, so just hear me out."

Before Samantha had a chance to start her tale, Zack jumped in. "A crazy guy came in here with a gun and started killing people. He was about to kill Samantha, but I stabbed him with some needles and he grew into a huge monster. We don't know where he is now, but we assume he still wants to kill us."

Watters looked at Zack incredulously.

"Oh, and he's wearing a cheap looking Santa Claus suit."

Watters looked back and forth between Zack and Samantha, searching for some hint that this was a joke. "Okay, this is a joke, right?" You don't expect me to believe there's a monster wearing a Santa suit running around the hospital, do you?"

"Not really," Samantha answered. "But it's the truth." She turned to Zack and glared at him. "I was going to explain the situation more delicately than Zack here did, as I know it's a lot to take in. But everything he said is true."

Watters looked at their faces again. "Okay, I don't know what the fuck is going on here, but you're both being weird. Were you doing the horizontal mambo in there, and you're trying to distract me with your crazy stories now that I found you?"

Zack blushed, even though he knew they did nothing wrong.

"No, you stupid asshole," Samantha shot back at him. "I told you … oh shit." She stopped speaking and stared over Dr. Watters's shoulder. At the far end of the hallway, the 'ding' of elevator doors opening could be heard.

"What's the matter," Watters quipped. "Afraid someone else is going to find out about you shagging the patients?"

Samantha ignored his comments, focusing on the elevator. The doors opened, revealing the Santa Beast.

"Oh fuck," she said.

"Shit, he found us," Zack chimed in. "Let's get out of here."

"Okay, cut the bullshit," Watters said, turning around to face what he assumed was anything other than an actual Santa Claus monster. When he saw there was indeed a strange looking person in a Santa suit, or at least part of one, he was surprised.

"Well, I'll be a monkey's dick," he said. "I still don't believe any of the other shit you were trying to feed me, but I admit that he does look like a creepo, at least from here."

"I don't care if you believe us or not," Samantha said. "Let's just get out of here, like Zack said."

In the distance, the monster smiled and began lumbering towards the arguing trio.

"Did you call the police," Watters asked casually, looking back at Samantha and seemingly not concerned in the least with the approaching menace.

"I tried, but you know how the service in this place is," Samantha answered.

"Of course," Watters responded. "But it doesn't help that you have a piece of shit phone."

"Jesus fucking Christ! Who cares what kind of phone I have? We need to get out of here. Now!"

The Santa Beast continued to close the gap between them, moving faster now.

"You two lovebirds can go and make out somewhere if you want. I'll take care of this guy." And with that, Dr. Watters turned and began walking towards the abnormal Santa Claus.

23

NO MATCH FOR SANTA

Dr. Watters strode up to the Santa Beast with what appeared to be all the confidence in the world, at least from Zack's standpoint.

What the hell's the matter with this guy, Zack thought. Does he not see what I see?

Zack wasn't sure, but he thought the monster was bigger than when he last saw him.

He has confidence, I'll give him that, Zack's thoughts continued. You could have used some of that confidence a few minutes ago when you had a chance to kiss Samantha. Then maybe you really *would* have been doing the "horizontal mambo" with her.

Yeah, right. In reality, you would have just been a dick like the guy in front of you marching to his probable death.

But who knows? The doctor does look like he's pretty fit. Maybe he can take him.

As Watters neared the monster, he began shouting at him. "Hey, loser, what the hell are you doing here? If you know what's good for you, you'll turn around and get the fuck out of this hospital. The police are on their way, and I might just decide to beat the shit out of you before they get here anyway."

Good grief, Zack thought. He's even a dick to the monster.

Would it be wrong to root for Santa in this instance?

The Santa Beast stopped, tilting his head as he looked at the cocky man coming towards him. Zack couldn't help but think of Michael Myers looking at Jamie Lee Curtis right before he decided he was there to kill her and anyone else who got in the way. Only this was real, and the Santa Beast was ten times more menacing than the white-masked movie killer.

Watters showed no such hesitation. He strode right up to the creature, only about a foot now separating them. The monster was a good foot taller than Dr. Watters, but the doctor didn't seem intimidated by the size difference.

Or the fact that he was facing off against a monstrous fucking beast, Zack thought.

"Okay, dipshit," Watters said, "I admit, the costume you got on is pretty good. Not sure where you came up with the idea, but it's realistic, I'll give you that. Well, realistic for a monster, anyway."

The Santa Beast straightened his head and looked directly at Dr. Watters's face.

"So here's the deal," Watters continued, jabbing a finger into the beast's chest. "We can do this the easy way or the hard way."

The Santa Beast looked down at the finger touching his rock hard pecs. With speed that belied his massive girth, his head shot down in a flash, and he chomped down on Watters's finger, amputating it with one bite.

"Holy fucking shit," the doctor screamed in a high pitched voice. Blood spurted out onto the Santa Beast's chest from the newly formed stump. He chewed up the finger for a few seconds before spitting it back into Dr. Watters's face.

As Watters stared wide-eyed at his mutilated finger, the Santa

Beast grabbed him by the genitals with one hand and his neck with the other. He lifted him over his head with ease and held him in the air for a few seconds, looking over at Samantha. He smiled.

Is he trying to impress her, Zack wondered.

This is fucked up on so many levels.

The Santa Beast turned back to the matter at hand. He hurled Watters forward, his body slamming against the wall. Watters was now gibbering incoherent sounds as he fell to the floor.

The beast took a deep breath, his muscular chest visibly rising. He grunted and moved forward to the whimpering doctor. He reached down and picked him up by the feet. He raised his arms, lifting Watters off of the ground before slamming him back down. Watters's head made impact with the floor, breaking apart like a perverted piñata.

Watters's body began to twitch as the Santa Beast repeated the process of picking him up by his feet and slamming him down on his head. By the second blow, Watters had stopped moving completely, and by the third, his head was no longer recognizable as a human body part. Brain bits coated the wall, some of them slowly oozing downward. Blood and gore covered the floor.

The Santa Beast held the doctor's lifeless body in front of him. He shook him a few times, hoping to get some reaction from his victim. However, he soon realized that his plaything was dead. He growled at the corpse, repositioned his hands so that one was holding his leg and the other was shoved into the pulpy mess that was once a handsome head. He rooted around, forcing his hand further into the corpse's body until he found something to latch on to. He then started to pull in opposite directions.

Good god, what is he doing, Zack thought.

And why the hell are we standing here watching it?

As if on cue, Samantha began to back away. She reached out, touching Zack's arm as she did so, prompting him to move along with her. But, much like a horrific traffic accident, they couldn't totally take their eyes off of the slaughter before them.

The Santa Beast continued to pull the dead doctor from both ends. At first, nothing happened. But he repositioned his hands, getting a good grip on the body parts. He took a deep breath and pulled again, growling as he did so. The bloody corpse began to stretch, followed by an audible ripping sound.

The doctor was literally being torn apart.

Once the separation of body parts started, it didn't take long for the beast to complete the process. The body split in two right along the ribcage. Blood poured onto the hospital floor, followed by long strings of floppy intestines. More internal organs came out in the waterfall of gore as well, but they were tougher to distinguish due to the amount of blood flowing out.

The Santa Beast held the two pieces of Dr. Watters up, looking at one, then the other. He smiled, but soon lost interest, tossing the two body halves back over his shoulders.

He then looked back at Samantha and Zack.

The Santa Beast licked his lips.

Zack and Samantha turned and ran.

The beast followed.

24

IT'S ABOUT TIME

Officer Fred Jones arrived at the hospital at 11:00 exactly. It was only a little more than an hour before his shift was over when the call came in. A late night dog walker had noises coming from the hospital. Probably nothing, but it needed to be checked out nevertheless.

So here he was. An hour to go until Christmas, and he was stuck investigating a potential shooting situation.

Sure seems quiet, he thought as "Dominic the Donkey" hee-hawed through the end of the holiday song on his radio.

Jones felt that the relative peace and quiet was a good sign. After all, if there really was some kind of incident, especially a shooting incident, there would probably be some type of activity outside of the building. That was typically how this kind of thing worked. At least from his twelve years of experience on the force. And unfortunately, he had seen quite a lot of shootings during his tenure as a police officer.

But he had also seen a hell of a lot more false alarms than actual incidents, so arriving to a quiet hospital on Christmas Eve filled him with hope.

Unless they're all already dead.

Way to keep up the positive thinking, he thought. But he knew that he needed to be prepared for anything. That was something they drilled into you during the academy. Don't take anything for granted, and always be prepared.

And on top of that, the craziest shit seemed to happen on the holidays. He didn't know why, but he had heard enough stories (and seen enough firsthand) to know that it was true. Maybe it was because it was the most depressing time of the year for so many. Or maybe it was because some asshole rich kid snapped when he didn't get what he wanted for Christmas.

Who knows, Jones thought. But hopefully none of those things are the case tonight. You can wrap up your Christmas Eve shift in an hour, get back home to your beautiful wife, and have some eggnog by the fire.

And maybe an early Christmas present if you're lucky.

The images he conjured in his mind brought a smile to his lips. Especially the last one.

But first things first, he told himself. Need to take care of business here, and then you can take care of business at home.

He had his pick of parking spaces, so he pulled into one in the front of the lot. Being an officer of the law, he could easily have simply pulled up to the curb in front of the hospital, but he didn't like to do that kind of thing. There was already enough distrust between citizens and the police these days, and he didn't want to do anything to further that way of thinking. Not that parking a few yards further back was going to make up for the shooting of unarmed men, but it wouldn't hurt. And he could only do what he could do.

He parked the car and turned off the ignition, silencing Andy

Williams in the midst of his signature song. The most wonderful time of the year indeed, Jones thought.

He got out of the patrol car and looked around. Nothing seemed to be out of the ordinary. It was quiet, but that in and of itself wasn't necessarily peculiar.

He started walking towards the entrance of the hospital, his boots crunching the freshly fallen snow. Just in the fifteen minutes it took him to arrive at his destination, the precipitation had really picked up, and it was beginning to accumulate.

Just an hour to go, he kept telling himself. Let's hope nothing is going on here, and then you can head home to Brenda. She'll have some wine glasses ready for you, and maybe she'll have that little see through teddy on.

Thinking about what awaited him at home (or what he *hoped* awaited him), he picked up his pace, arriving at the entrance to the hospital in just a few seconds. The automatic doors slid open as he approached, and he entered the hospital.

25

GOING UP?

Zack and Samantha reached the stairwell door, and Samantha surged ahead and slammed into it with her palms. The door shot open, and they raced into the stairwell.

Although there had been no time to discuss or coordinate, both Samantha and Zack had individually determined that they would head down the stairs, get off at the next floor down, and race over to the elevator where they could go the rest of the way down. Unfortunately, their passage to the ground floor was once again blocked off.

"Mother fucker," Samantha hollered, seeing the new blockade. Similar to the initial barricade set up a few floors down, there were hospital carts strewn about in such a way as to make the voyage down impossible. At least, not possible in time to avoid the hulking monster that was heading their way.

"He works fast, I'll give him that," Zack said.

"Yeah, kudos to him," Samantha replied. "Come on, I guess we're going up."

"Up?" Zack questioned. "I thought we were already on the top floor."

"We are," Samantha answered.

"Oh, shit," Zack muttered as he followed Samantha up the stairs.

26

REINFORCEMENTS, PLEASE

Officer Jones surveyed the lobby of the hospital. Pretty impressive for a smallish hospital, he thought.

Similar to what he experienced outside, everything was quiet. And again, this reassured him a bit. After all, you can't have a mass shooting in silence.

But just because there wasn't someone running around with a machine gun, that didn't mean everything was perfect. Although mass shootings seemed to be all the rage these days, it was possible to walk into a crime scene that didn't involve heavy gun fire or numerous casualties. In fact, that was the most likely case. And one he'd rather not encounter if need be.

But either way, he needed to be prepared. He kept his gun holstered, but remained on the alert in case a quick draw was needed.

Okay, so the good news is that you don't hear an uzi mowing down innocent people, Jones thought. But it's almost *too* quiet. Shouldn't there be something going on down here? Some idle chatter, or the clickety-click of a keyboard?

It *is* pretty late on Christmas Eve, he thought. Maybe it will actually be a quiet Christmas for once. Maybe the call about a shooting was just a prank or a false alarm.

You can only hope, he decided. And maybe you can get home soon and the missus will be wearing that "sexy Mrs. Claus" suit she bought a few years back.

Jones couldn't hold back the smile. It wasn't just the image of his wife that made him smile, but the idea that costume designers made a "sexy" version of pretty much every possible thing. Growing up, he had never thought of Mrs. Claus as being a sex symbol, or really even attractive in any fashion. She was a fat old lady. And she surely didn't wear a short little red coat and high heeled boots when getting Santa ready for his sleigh ride. But some costume manufacturer had decided she did, and Jones wasn't complaining.

Okay, back to the task at hand, he thought.

He moved further into the hospital, looking for any signs of life. He saw what appeared to be the front desk, and moved towards it.

Doesn't appear to be anyone manning the desk, he mentally noted. He continued on regardless.

As he closed the distance between himself and the front desk, the realization hit him that something wasn't right. This wasn't an "everything's okay" silence.

It was the opposite.

A "something's fucked up" silence.

He hoped he was wrong. But he had always had good instincts. And he had been a cop long enough to know to trust those instincts.

He quickened his pace, keeping alert to the surrounding area. His gun was still holstered, but the palm of his hand now rested on the butt of his weapon. He kept hoping a receptionist or some hospital staff would pop up from behind the desk to tell him everything was fine. There was no need for the police, and he could go home to his beautiful wife.

But that didn't happen.

Jones reached the desk. Still nothing. He didn't want to call out, in case there truly was something nefarious going on. It's not typically a good strategy to alert the criminals of your presence.

He put his hands on the desk and leaned forward, standing on his toes to peer over the desk.

"Sweet Jesus." The words escaped his lips as he peered down at the two bloody corpses. He thumbed the call button on his walkie talkie, simultaneously pulling his firearm from its holster. After identifying himself and his location, he provided the details. "I have two dead civilians here. Both appear to be hospital staff and were shot in the head. Requesting immediate backup." He pushed the button again, silencing his responders. He knew the drill. They'd tell him to stand his ground while he waited for reinforcements to arrive.

But he also knew that that meant more people could die before backup arrived.

Looks like sexy Mrs. Claus is going to wait a little longer than anticipated, he thought as he held his gun out at the ready and walked further into the hospital.

27

THE ROOF

Samantha burst out onto the roof, with Zack following close behind. The cold air slammed into them, Zack feeling the worst of it. In only his hospital gown and socks, he was definitely not dressed for gallivanting around the rooftops on a blustery winter night. But he tried to suck it up as best he could. Aside from the fact that there were more urgent threats presumably coming up behind him, he also didn't want to look like a wimp in front of Samantha.

"Now what," Zack asked. He had to shout to be heard over the howling wind.

"I don't know," Samantha said as she looked around the rooftop. "I'm making this up as I go along."

Samantha didn't have a brilliant plan in mind when she led the way up to the roof. She simply knew it was the only way to go to get away from Jared. But she was hoping that there would be someplace to hide, or that there would be something she could use in their battle against the monster.

But that did not appear to be the case.

The roof was flat, with a few mechanical structures placed throughout. Chimneys, generators, things like that. Nothing that could be used to fight against the Santa Beast. And probably not big enough to hide them from him, either.

Hell, he seemed to be superhuman at this point, Samantha thought. His physical strength has sure as hell increased, but his senses seemed to as well. It was almost as if he knew where she and Zack were going before they did.

She looked back at Zack, who had his arms wrapped around himself in a feeble attempt to keep warm. He was visibly shivering.

This is great, Samantha thought. If Jared somehow doesn't find us up here, we'll die from hypothermia. Although dressed slightly warmer than Zack, Samantha was still feeling the effects of the cold, and she knew they couldn't stay out here much longer.

And she also knew that her fantasies of Jared not finding them were pretty unrealistic as well.

On cue with Samantha's thoughts, a loud blast was heard from the direction of the doorway that they had just emerged from. Zack and Samantha both turned their heads to the sound, knowing what they would see. And as expected, there stood the Santa Beast, the shattered door laying at his feet.

He had kicked out the door and now stood there, breathing deeply and audibly. He reminded Samantha of a bull, getting ready to charge the matador.

Only in this case, she and Zack didn't have the "fight" rigged like a matador typically would. And they sure as hell weren't facing just a bull.

They began to back away from the hulking monstrosity.

The Santa Beast grunted and started forward.

28

ROOFTOP FIGHT

"**P**lease tell me there's another way back down that you just thought of," Zack said to Samantha as the two of them backed away from the quickly approaching monster.

"I just thought of another way down," Samantha responded.

"Really?"

"No."

"Okay, great."

They were both getting colder by the second, but Zack was suffering the worst. Standing in the snow with only his hospital socks to protect him from the elements, his feet were already starting to go numb.

And he was rapidly losing hope.

Okay, I'm definitely back to my original thought that this Christmas sucks, he thought.

"Come on," Samantha said, grabbing his arm and pulling him away from the monster looming before them. The contact from Samantha revived him for the moment, and he found the strength to get moving. Zack slipped and began to fall down, his heart seemingly stopping for a second, as he knew he was about to die. But Samantha held tight to him, and he was able to maintain his balance. Together, they hustled over to one of the heating units and stood behind it, giving them at least a minimal barrier from their enemy.

The impediment barely slowed the beast down at all. He continued his march towards his targets. Once reaching the heating unit, he grasped it with both hands and began to pull. It only took a few seconds for the structure to begin tearing away from its foundation. Nuts and bolts and pieces of metal broke apart as the unit was lifted from the roof and tossed aside.

Jesus Christ, he's getting stronger, Zack thought. A few minutes ago, he had trouble tearing a person apart (which is no small feat in and of itself). Now he tore up a heating unit as if it was nothing.

The Santa Beast looked back at Zack and Samantha after ridding himself of the large structure that was blocking his path to them. He smiled and said something which was hard to decipher through his garbled voice. But Zack was pretty sure he was saying Samantha's name.

"We're fucked," Zack said to Samantha. They both began to back away from the monster, but there wasn't much room before they would reach the side of the building.

"I tend to agree with you," Samantha said. They clasped hands and continued moving back until they were as far as they could go before plummeting five floors to the ground below.

The Santa Beast, seeing that they had run out of room, smiled. He started to advance on them.

"There's nowhere for us to run anymore," Samantha said to Zack. Her voice was flat, and she sounded resigned to her fate. "And I'm not going out like Watters."

"What are you saying?" Zack said, turning to face her.

Samantha didn't say another word, but simply clutched Zack's hand tighter as she looked into his eyes. She didn't need to say anything further for Zack to understand what she was thinking.

Zack looked back to the Santa Beast. He was taking his time, seemingly enjoying having them trapped, but still closing the distance. Zack looked behind him, viewing the long trek to the ground floor. And then he looked back at Samantha.

God, she was beautiful.

"Fuck this shit," Zack said. He let go of Samantha's hand and turned towards his nemesis once again. "Hey, you ugly bastard. Come and get me." He raced along the edge of the building, putting some distance between himself and Samantha.

The Santa Beast looked a bit confused as he followed Zack's path away from Samantha. He cocked his head, then appeared to lose interest, and turned back to Samantha. He took another step forward.

Okay, that didn't work out as planned, Zack thought. Guess he's more interested in her than me.

I can understand why, but I was hoping he wouldn't be able to resist chasing me, and giving Samantha a chance to make a break for it.

But of course he would choose her over you, idiot. You would, too.

Plus, he's obsessed with her.

That's it!

"Hey, shithead," Zack started again, louder this time. "While we were running away from you before, I had sex with your girlfriend there."

The Santa Beast turned back towards Zack.

So did Samantha.

Sorry, Zack thought. He wasn't sure if Samantha was more pissed at him for running off and trying to be a hero or lying about having sex with her. He assumed the former, but actually felt more embarrassed by the latter.

Fighting Santa Claus monsters and probably going to die in a few minutes, yet you still get embarrassed by the same kinds of mundane things.

Either way, the comments seemed to do the trick, at least temporarily. The Santa Beast turned away from Samantha and glared at Zack. They looked at each other for a few seconds before the monster turned back to Samantha.

The beast took another step towards her.

Samantha backed up as well. She was now teetering on the edge of the building.

Shit, Zack thought. I don't have time for this.

Sorry, Samantha.

"Hey, you ugly fucker," he shouted back at the creature. "Didn't you hear what I just said? I had sex with Samantha. A bunch of times. And she told me how much better it was with me than with you."

The Santa Beast stopped and turned back toward the direction of the insults. He stared at Zack, his expression angrier than before.

Come on, Zack thought. Come get me you piece of shit. Back away from Samantha already.

The creature stared at him but didn't move. Zack noticed Samantha glancing behind her, peering down the side of the building.

Fuck it. "Not only did we have sex a bunch of times, but she told me it was great to be with a real man after being with you, and that I was ten times bigger than you."

The Santa Beast growled, turning his whole body towards Zack. He then started moving towards him.

Despite everything, Zack couldn't help but chuckle at the situation. Nothing like mocking a guy's manhood to get him angry. Even a Santa Claus monster.

But the monster's quickness took Zack by surprise. Zack didn't expect someone so huge to be able to move so fast. Perhaps it was whatever drugs he had injected into him – maybe they made him faster as well as stronger. Maybe it was the galoshes he wore as part of his Santa costume that gave him good traction. Either way, Zack didn't have the benefit of either of these things, so when he moved to evade the charging behemoth, his feet, which were now completely numb from standing in the snow, lost their purchase. They slipped out from under him and he toppled over into the snow.

The disturbed snow barely had time to settle around him before Zack felt claw-like hands grab him by the hospital gown, with a good chunk of his skin going along for the ride. He then felt himself being lifted up, and a few seconds later, hurled through the air. He barely had time to process what was happening before his head struck the brick wall that encapsulated the stairwell from which they had emerged onto the roof.

Zack fell back into the fluffy snow, although this time barely cognizant of where he lay. He wasn't unconscious, but he felt as though he was on his way to that state.

The one thought that did creep its way into his addled brain was how he had been airborne for so long a journey. *Did he really throw me practically all the way across the roof?* He reached out to feel his head, mostly to make sure it was still attached to his body. The good news was that it was. The bad news was that the functioning part of it sensed a presence standing over him.

A second later, Zack was yanked up by his surgically repaired wrist. The cast was crushed from the pressure of the monster's grip, and Zack's wrist was crushed along with it. He was pulled up with such force that it caused his shoulder to dislocate. Zack let out a shriek at the piercing pain, but it was quickly cut short as the wind was knocked out of him from a powerful blow to the midsection delivered by the Santa Beast.

In excruciating agony from both the wrist and shoulder injuries, and now gasping for breath, Zack was picked up by his throat. The Santa Beast easily gripped him by the neck and picked him up with one arm, choking him as he did so. The abomination's claws dug into his skin at the same time, causing blood to dribble out and form along the cup of the beast's hand where it gripped Zack's throat.

Guess this is it, Zack thought as he started to lose consciousness.

Just before everything went black, the last vestiges of Zack's mind still functioning noticed someone else emerge through the ruined doorway and onto the roof.

29

A CHRISTMAS NIGHTMARE

"Holy fucking shit," Officer Jones muttered as he caught his first glimpse of the Santa Beast. He was clearly seeing a monstrous creature in a tattered Santa suit strangling a young man, but his mind was having trouble processing this information.

What the hell did I walk into?

Although not fully accepting what he was looking at, he was able to understand the fact that whatever this thing was, it was killing one of the hospital's patients. Perhaps he was already dead. Either way, Jones knew he had to do something, and his veteran police instincts kicked in.

"Drop him, asshole," he shouted, raising his gun at the monster.

The Santa Beast looked over at the new participant in their rooftop melodrama and smiled.

Jesus Christ, that's one ugly motherfucker, Jones thought.

"I said drop him. Now!"

Surprisingly, the beast in the Santa outfit did what the officer requested, although with a bit more gusto than Jones would have preferred. He threw Zack to the side, his lifeless body landing precariously close to the building's edge. His ruined arm lay at an odd angle, and he showed no signs of movement.

Wasn't expecting that, Jones thought.

Now what? I somehow doubt he's going to let me take him in to the station for questioning.

The beast turned to fully face the policeman and began moving forward. Jones was about to tell him to stop, but he knew that would be a pointless exercise. Whatever this thing was, it surely wasn't human, at least not in the typical sense. And he certainly wasn't going to comply with anymore of the officer's requests.

Jones fired his weapon repeatedly, emptying his clip into the beast. The monster staggered backwards a step or two, but stayed upright. He looked down at his chest where all of the bullets had impacted him. His head shot back up, his eyes boring into those of Officer Jones.

"Fuck me," Jones mumbled as the beast advanced on him in such a quick strike that he had no chance to evade the attack. The Santa Beast grabbed Jones's arm with both of his hands, raised it in the air, then slammed it down over his knee, breaking it in half. Jones let out an ear splitting scream, spittle flying from his mouth. The beast let go of the fractured limb. Half of the arm hung loosely by the policeman's side, connected only by some flaps of skin that had managed to hold. Jagged white bone could be seen poking out of both halves of the arm.

As Officer Jones continued to cry out, disbelieving what was happening to him, the Santa Beast grabbed him by the throat with one hand and the groin with the other. He lifted the policeman over his head and walked over to the side of the building.

Through the pain and shock of what was transpiring, Jones could detect that there was increased activity down on the ground from when he had first arrived at the hospital. The familiar sight of police sirens flashing and officers milling about registered in his brain.

About time, he thought, knowing that they were too late to help him.

As he was thrown from the top of the building, his final thoughts as he plummeted through the harsh winter air were of his wife whom he would never see again.

30

OH MY, THE SNOW IS GETTNG HEAVY!

Officers Quigley and Terashita were the first to arrive at the hospital after Jones's call for backup. They were two of the younger members of the force, which made them both wonder why they had been partnered together. Maybe it was because no one else wanted to be partnered with one of the only two women officers. Even in this day and age, sexism was rampant, especially in the law enforcement environment. Or perhaps it was because there was no real need for a veteran from the force to be teamed with the younger officers. After all, there wasn't much crime in their jurisdiction, and most of their time was spent sitting around waiting for something to happen. And when they did get a call, it usually ended up to be a false alarm or a situation that didn't need much more attention that the presence of someone in uniform to straighten everyone out.

They pulled up to the side of the hospital building. Terashita, who was driving the police car, turned off the ignition but left the lights flashing. She looked over at her partner.

"Okay, what now?" she asked.

Quigley, who was looking at herself in her compact mirror, shrugged. "Beats me. I guess we get out and fight crime."

"What the fuck are you doing?" Terashita snapped. "Put that thing away for Christ's sake. Who are you trying to impress?"

Quigley looked over at her partner, one eyebrow raised. "Do I really need to tell you?"

Terashita rolled her eyes. "First of all, Officer Jones is the one who called for backup. I'm guessing he's a little busy for your attempts to pick him up."

Quigley ignored her partner's rational words and was now adjusting her bosom under her tight fitting uniform.

"And second," Terashita continued, "he's married."

Quigley looked over at Terashita again. "Really? When did that ever make a difference?"

"You're hopeless," Terashita responded, rolling her eyes once more. Being teamed with Quigley, it felt like a continuous motion.

"Hopelessly *horny*," Quigley said cheerily.

"Okay, I can see you're not going to be any help," Terashita said.

Now Quigley was the one who rolled her eyes. "Don't get your panties in a bunch," she said to her partner. Let's just wait until the rest of our backup arrives. We can follow their lead."

"Is that what we're supposed to do?"

"How the hell would I know?"

"That's true. During training, you basically spent all of your time hitting on that one guy. Jay or something."

"Yeah," Quigley sighed. "He was nice. Too bad he got kicked off the force."

"He was a meth head."

"Yeah, but he was a great lay."

A few seconds of silence filled the patrol car before Terashita spoke up. "Okay, you can sit here and wait for help, but I'm going to check things out. I want to at least *look* like I'm trying to do my job." She unbuckled her seatbelt and reached for the door handle when the body of Officer Jones smashed into the car's windshield. The dead officer's head poked through the shattered glass, his body a mangled heap outside of the vehicle.

Terashita and Quigley screamed in unison. The sound of police sirens was approaching.

Quigley decided to join her partner outside of the police car.

31

SANTA DOESN'T TAKE 'NO' FOR AN ANSWER!

The same line kept repeating itself in Samantha's head. *I can't believe this is happening.*

Watching the monster that she once knew as Jared throw the officer off the roof through the swirling snowfall was surreal. My ex-boyfriend has literally become a monster, and he just threw a police officer off of a building.

I can't believe this is happening.

But it *was* happening. And now that Jared had disposed of the policeman and Zack, he was sure to turn his attention back to her.

Zack had bought her a few minutes, probably even saved her life for the moment (and now he may be lying dead over there), but she had squandered the opportunity.

No, she thought. Not squandered. Simply not many choices.

Even if she had been able to evade Jared and run back into the hospital, she couldn't just leave Zack behind. He just risked (gave?) his life for her. She couldn't just leave him on the roof to fend for himself.

But now he's probably dead or dying, and you just stood there, so you're going to die now, too. So his sacrifice was totally wasted.

Fuck it, she thought. There weren't any good options here. It is what it is. You're still here, and you have to deal with the situation at hand.

Maybe there's still time, Samantha thought. Jared seems pretty mesmerized with the man he just murdered. If he stays distracted for just a few more seconds, maybe you can scoot by him, get out of this goddam hospital and get help. You'd feel like a shit for leaving Zack, but let's be honest, it's pretty much the only chance either of you have for surviving the night.

Just as Samantha was gearing up for an actual attempt to make it off the roof, the Santa Beast turned his head back towards her.

There goes that plan.

The menacing brute began walking towards her. Samantha considered trying to make a break for it anyway, but she knew it would be pointless. There wasn't that much room on the roof as it was, and she had seen the monster in action. For a hulking beast, he was quick as the devil.

The beast stopped a few feet in front of Samantha. He looked into her eyes.

Are you still in there, Jared?

He opened his mouth, but nothing came out.

"Jared," Samantha said, "why are you doing this?" Stupid question, she knew, but she was desperate. She didn't know how much of Jared was even still inside of the monster staring at her. And he hadn't exactly been the nicest guy before he turned into the Santa Beast anyway. Hell, she didn't even know if he physically could talk anymore.

The creature opened his mouth again. He looked as though he wanted to say something, but he was clearly struggling.

"It's okay, Jared," Samantha continued. "We have all night." She tried to remain calm, but she knew damn well that they did not have all night. Especially Zack.

"Subanta," finally came out of the monster's mouth.

He said my name. Sounded like shit, but he said my name.

It wasn't much, but it gave Samantha the tiniest shred of hope. At least some part of his brain was still human. Maybe he could be reasoned with.

"Don you unerstan thad we were mean do be dogedder?"

"Jared, you have to stop this. I don't know what happened to you, but if I did anything to lead you on--." She was interrupted by a guttural roar coming from the man beast standing before her.

Okay, that doesn't seem like a good sign.

"If I can't have you, no one will," the monster screamed as he walked towards her once more.

I heard *that* part pretty clearly, Samantha thought, as she backed away from the charging monster. Guess he feels strongly about that point.

She backed up just a few steps before she was back to the edge of the building. She had considered jumping a few minutes ago when it seemed hopeless. But she doubted she would have actually been able to do it. And she didn't think she could do it now.

But her options were pretty limited.

Before she had a chance to mull it over any further, the Santa Beast was upon her. He grabbed her simultaneously with both of his claw-like hands, one grasping her by the throat and the other latching onto her hair. He lifted her into the air, moving closer to the edge of the building.

Samantha began to choke as she was carried, but the hand pulling on her hair actually alleviated some of the pressure to her esophagus. She gasped for air, but wasn't being strangled enough to pass out and ultimately expire.

Doesn't matter, she thought through her gagging fits. If he

doesn't choke you to death, you're destined for a one way trip to the street below.

The behemoth stopped at the edge of building, holding Samantha over empty space. Samantha kicked her legs, instinctively trying to gain purchase with her feet. But it was no use. The Santa Beast's arms were too long, and she couldn't reach out far enough with her legs. And being choked surely didn't help anything.

If he let's go now, I'm dead, she knew. Nothing to grab onto, and nowhere to go but down.

He let go of her.

32

NOTHING LEFT TO DO

Zack regained consciousness just in time to see the freakish Santa Claus advancing on Samantha. Between the excruciating pain emanating from his detached shoulder and destroyed wrist, the wooziness from lack of oxygen to his brain, the loss of feeling in certain body parts due to the cold, and the increasing winds and snowfall, it wasn't the clearest sight he had ever viewed. However, he was with it enough to tell that Samantha was in big trouble.

The memory of his attempted heroic deeds played in his addled mind. At least it wasn't totally pointless, he thought. Samantha's still alive.

Yeah, but not for long.

Gotta do something. But what?

Things didn't go quite so well last time you faced off against him...

Now he's got Samantha cornered, and you're in way worse shape than a few minutes ago.

Face it, you're fucked.

Probably, Zack knew. But sitting her whining about it isn't doing any good. You're not dead yet.

First thing's first. Stand the hell up.

Purposely not using his dislocated arm, Zack began the attempt of rising to his feet. But even the slightest movement sent stabs of pain through his entire body. He almost passed out again, but forced himself to hold it together. He managed to get up on one knee before he had to pause to refocus.

He glanced back to the scene playing out by the rooftop's edge. The Santa Beast was closer to Samantha now, and it sounded like they were talking to each other, but Zack couldn't make out what they were saying.

Is that a positive sign?

Fat chance, he knew. Even if the creature miraculously reverted back to his normal self, he wasn't going to simply apologize and make nice with everyone.

If he's saying anything, it's probably just describing how he plans to kill all of us!

And then, as if to act on Zack's sarcastic thoughts, he witnessed the beast lunge towards Samantha and grasp her by the head.

Jesus Christ, he's going to twist her head off!

Zack watched as he ruthlessly brought Samantha to the side of the building, Samantha's legs pinwheeling as she was hauled over.

This isn't going to end well, Zack thought.

But what can you do?

It was bad enough just trying to stand up. What chance would he have of overpowering the monstrous Santa (if he could even make it over to them) and avoid having Samantha plummet to her death? Even if he found a way to surprise the beast, Samantha was in a quite precarious situation.

And if you don't do something, he thought, it looks like he's going to drop her off the building anyway.

Face it, Zack old boy. You're fucked.

And then, as if to punctuate that thought, he watched the monster drop her.

33

NOT DEAD YET

What do you know, Samantha thought with an odd clarity as she began her plummet to the ground beneath her. Your life really does flash before your eyes.

Fortunately for her, it didn't get very far before the Santa Beast ended her brief descent by grabbing hold of her hair.

Although barely able to grasp what was transpiring, her natural survival instinct made her relieved to no longer be falling. But the pain that radiated in her scalp made it difficult to be truly satisfied with her situation. She honestly didn't know how her hair didn't completely rip out of her head. That being said, she was pretty sure she heard some tearing sounds.

But it held.

Awesome. You get to live for a few more seconds anyway.

The Santa Beast pulled her up by one arm. He raised her high enough so that she was eye level with him. He was smiling at her, although Samantha didn't notice due to the pain induced tears that were welling up in her eyes.

The Santa Beast grunted something unintelligible. Samantha couldn't understand what he was saying. She blinked and tried to focus on his face, but this didn't help. Although it did look like he was enjoying himself. She was pretty certain that any chance she may have had of reasoning her way out of this was long gone. At this point, she guessed that even pledging to run off with him and be his sex slave for life wouldn't have saved her ass.

He's just going to dangle me here for as long as it give him his jollies, she thought through the pain. *And then you're dead. He'll either drop you (for real this time), or maybe pull you back in and rape you and probably eat you.*

As she thought about the different ways she may perish at the hands of her ex beau, something caught her eye over his shoulder.

It was Zack, and he was standing up.

For a second, she felt hope for her own survival. But that quickly washed away. Zack wouldn't be crazy enough to try to save her again. Would he?

Doesn't matter, she knew. *Even if he was that selfless a person, it wouldn't do any good. He would be just as ineffective as he was the first time. Probably more so, due to his weakened condition. And Jared's seemingly increasing strength and savagery.*

Just get out of here while you can, she thought regarding Zack. *It's been a hell of a night, and you're a good guy. Kind of cute, too. If things had been different...*

34

GOT 'IM!

It took less than a minute for all hell to break loose in the hospital parking lot.

At least that's what it felt like to Officer Terashita. One minute she and Quigley were discussing what exactly they should be doing (with Quigley more concerned with her makeup), and the next there was a dead body on top of their patrol car and what seemed like the entire police force milling about with their hair on fire. Terashita didn't realize there were even this many people *on* the force in their local little town.

But despite all of the hustle and bustle surrounding them, nothing was actually being accomplished. It reminded Terashita of that dumb black and white sitcom her mom used to watch – the episode where the crazy lady was having a baby, and despite the husband and friends planning everything out ahead of time, they all went crazy when the time actually came.

To her credit (and somewhat surprising herself), Terashita tried to keep everyone focused. Despite the dead policeman on top of her car, there was still a situation in the hospital. And, apparently, on *top* of the hospital. After all, Officer Jones didn't just end up on the hospital roof by magic. And she seriously doubted that he had committed suicide.

There's someone else up there.

But no one on the ground seemed to care. Every time Terashita tried to talk to her fellow officers, all of whom were her seniors and theoretically more experienced in these types of situations, she was dismissively brushed aside. The few times an officer did pay attention to her, they were not focusing on the words coming out of her mouth.

And her partner was sure as hell no use. Not that she was super helpful in the first place when it came to official police business, but as soon as the body of their fellow officer smashed into their car, Quigley completely lost it. She was running around raving to the other officers who had since arrived, and that simply added to the overall chaos of the situation.

Fuck it, Terashita said to herself. This is your chance to prove yourself. While all of the men are running around doing nothing (except for occasionally fawning over your big breasted partner), you can take charge and handle the situation.

Sometimes, if you need a job done right, send in a woman!

Okay, she thought, happy with her decision to take charge. Now what?

She didn't have long to think about it before she spied Samantha dangling from the roof of the hospital.

"Holy shit, there's someone hanging over the edge of the building," she shouted, pointing up to the scene of the crime. A few officers looked her way, but it was nothing more than a casual glance. And most ignored her altogether.

"Fucking assholes," Terashita muttered. She squinted, trying to better understand what she was looking at above. At first it looked like someone was levitating just off of the hospital's roof. But since they weren't falling to their death, something must have been holding them.

Something or someone.

But between the snowfall, the dark of night, and the distance from where Terashita herself stood, it was tough to say for certain what was going on. She backed up a few steps, trying to get a better vantage point.

Better, she thought. From where she now stood, it was clear that someone was indeed hanging over the edge. It appeared to be a woman. And the more she stared at the scene above, it was clear someone's arm was holding her where she frantically kicked her legs.

Terashita turned to her fellow officers to try once again to get their attention. She opened her mouth, but quickly shut it.

Fuck them, she thought. They've been no help so far, what makes you think they're going to help this time.

And besides, this can be your chance to prove yourself.

Terashita moved behind the patrol car that was parked just a few feet away. She pulled her weapon and crouched behind the car, her elbows resting on the hood and her gun aimed at the incident above.

Shit, this isn't good, Terashita thought as she took aim. At this distance, there's a good chance you're going to miss your target. And even if you don't, what's going to happen? He'll drop the victim and she'll go splat, just like Officer Jones.

Yeah, and if you don't do anything, you're probably going to get the same result.

No risk, no reward, she thought.

She closed one eye and extended her arms.

Here goes nothing.

She pulled the trigger.

35

HE'S HIT!

The sound of the gunshot jolted Zack, causing him to almost fall over.

Holy fuck, what now, he thought.

Too much happening at once. Getting nearly killed by Santa Beast over there. Samantha being dangled over the edge of the building. Being dropped off the building, only to be caught at the last second. And now another gunshot.

Shit, should be used to this by now, he thought.

As the shot sounded, his focus was directed towards the monster's head. It looked like something shot off of it. An ear perhaps?

Yes, Zack exclaimed internally. Maybe the good guys finally showed up, and they're taking down this fucking monster.

But what does that mean for Samantha, who's still dangling over the edge of the building?

The new fear barely formed in his head before he saw the Santa Beast's body spin the slightest bit. The shot hadn't taken him out, but it had apparently jolted him enough to force him to move with the impact of the bullet. And he luckily took Samantha with him before dropping her to the cold concrete of the hospital roof in order to clutch his destroyed ear.

Finally, something's going our way, Zack thought, new surges of adrenaline shooting through his body.

As if acting of its own accord, his body propelled itself forward, being fueled with the newfound energy generated from seeing Samantha saved, at least for the time being. He surely hadn't actively thought it was a good idea to launch another attack on the monster before him. Nor would he have even thought it possible, based on the current condition of his body. Not if he had been granted the opportunity to think it over, anyway.

But it didn't matter. This obviously wasn't a night of logical happenings or events based on preconceived scientific findings.

No, it was Christmas. The day for fucking miracles. And all kinds of other crazy shit, apparently.

He lunged toward his imposing enemy, who was grimacing and still holding the side of his head. So he *can* be hurt, Zack thought as he plowed into the beast with all of his strength. It was like running straight into a brick wall, and the good feelings that had entered Zack for a few seconds quickly disappeared.

He didn't fucking move at all!

No, that's not true, Zack thought. He did budge a tiny bit. Negligible, but he stumbled a few inches closer to the edge.

Hooray for you! You moved him maybe an inch after he was just shot and he wasn't prepared for your attack. Way to go.

And the adrenaline you were feeling a few seconds ago seems to have been turned off like a faucet.

The Santa Beast looked right at Zack, snarling. He removed his hand from the pulpy mess that had been his ear. Blood and goo dripped off the side of his head, some sticking to his hand.

Zack prepared for the worst. With basically no strength left and the monster's full attention on him, he knew he was done for.

Nice knowing you, Samantha. And sorry I didn't get to see those leather pants one more time, Nancy.

The Santa Beast started to reach out for Zack when the second shot rang out. Another explosion of blood, this time on the other side of his head.

Holy shit, Zack thought. His other ear just got blown off. Whoever's shooting at this asshole is either a fucking awesome shot or lucky as hell.

The Santa Beast pulled one of his arms back, clutching his newly afflicted wound. More goopy blood seeped out from between his fingers. The force of the bullet caused him to twist his body a bit. It wasn't much, but he was close enough to the edge of the building now that he lost his footing, causing him to stumble some more.

Alright, you mother fucking asshole. Fall already!

The evil Santa Claus teetered on the edge, but it looked to Zack like he was going to regain his footing.

Fuck this shit!

Zack shoved his arms forward, his open palms slamming into the beast's midsection. It was still basically like trying to knock over a brick wall, only this time, the massive wall was missing a brick or two. Barely anything, but enough to send the wall, or in this case, person (monster?), tumbling over.

It was slow at first, and for a moment, Zack thought it still wasn't enough. But the Santa Beast was simply too close to the edge, his body mass too great, his balance too off, and the laws of physics dictated that he needed to fall backward.

Hot shit, you did it!

Despite everything, a wave of euphoria spread through him.

The aches and pains were forgotten (partly due to the numbness brought on by the cold) as he reveled in his success.

The fucker was going down!

And then he realized that his nemesis was still clutching his hospital gown with one bloody hand.

Oh fuck.

36

GOING DOWN?

Zack knew he was a dead man. Sure, he had known this multiple times tonight, but this time, he *really* knew it. He was already falling over, following the Santa Beast over the side of the building. And he didn't see the creature losing his grip on the flimsy hospital gown – nothing was going to escape his vise-like grip.

Well, at least I'm taking this son of a bitch with me, Zack thought. Even *he* can't survive a fall from this height.

Right?

The descent over the side of the building accelerated. The Santa Beast was now more horizontal than vertical, and Zack was picking up speed. As he fell forward and his view of the street below came into view, Zack compared the feeling to that of going over the hill of a roller coaster. A really, really steep roller coaster. Only ten billion times more terrifying, and a much less pleasant stop at the end.

Funny the shit that goes through your head when you're about to bite the big one.

But before he went completely over the edge, he felt something touch his leg. At least he thought he felt something. His body was so ravaged and numb from his injuries and the cold at this point, that he wasn't sure what he was feeling.

He continued in a downward trajectory, but before he toppled over the edge of the building, his legs were jerked backward. It wasn't much, but it was enough so that more of his body connected with the roof than originally would have. It hurt like hell when he impacted, but he didn't immediately fall over the edge to his death.

Fortunately, the Santa Beast *did* continue his normal descent and flipped over the edge.

*Un*fortunately, he was still holding onto Zack.

Zack saw himself being pulled off of the building along with the monster, both of them plummeting to the ground and smashing into bloody bits. But for once, Zack was happy to only be wearing the flimsy hospital gown. It was no match for Santa Beast's size and strength. After only a few seconds of the two men looking into each other's eyes, hate burning in the orbs of the monster, the fabric of the gown gave way, and the holiday abomination fell into the swirling winds and out of sight below.

Holy shit, I'm alive, Zack thought. I'm fucking alive.

And naked.

Shivering even more from the cold now that he had absolutely nothing to protect him (except for his now completely soaked through hospital socks), he turned his head to see who or what had saved him from his untimely end. Holding onto his legs was Samantha.

"Nice butt," she said, smiling.

37

ANOTHER ONE?

The holiday horror plummeted down through the wintry weather like something out of a *Die Hard* movie.

With his newfound girth, he reached his destination rapidly. Not that his brain had much capacity to think logically anymore, but he barely had time to realize what was happening before he impacted the earth below. Unlike Officer Jones, the Santa Beast managed to miss all of the police cars, and instead smashed directly into the paved area of the hospital parking lot.

No one would be parking in that section for the foreseeable future.

He landed with such force that the blacktop broke apart at the point of impact. But the damage done to the creature's body was much worse. He landed head first, and his skull cracked open like an overripe melon. Blood and brain matter splashed some of the officers standing nearby. Once fully landed, the beast's body lay at multiple odd angles, the majority of his bones now broken.

. . .

ALL OF THE police officers stopped in their tracks upon the Santa Beast hitting the ground. Once they realized what had happened, most of them continued either staring at the fallen monster, or they looked around as if searching for what they should do about it. A select few, including one especially burly officer, began to freak out, as he was one of the unfortunate victims of the creature's splattering. He ran in small circles for a few seconds before running off into the night.

Terashita smiled at the officer's overreaction. For the life of her she couldn't remember his name, but she absolutely remembered the time he had tried to hit on her while simultaneously making a racist remark. It was quite satisfying to see him exposed in front of everyone for the loser that he was.

But better than the asshole cop running away was the fact that she apparently took down whatever this thing was. She didn't know exactly what transpired up on the roof, but she was pretty sure that she hit the beast with her shots, and she also knew that no one else fell off of the building. She couldn't guarantee that the woman he had been dangling over the edge was still okay up there, but at least she hadn't fallen to her death like this thing did.

She had taken action. And it looked like she was successful.

Maybe she'd get a little respect from now on.

She took a closer look at the thing that had fallen to the ground. What the hell is that, she wondered. She walked closer to it, trying to determine what she was looking at. At first, she thought it was just a really large man, but as she got closer, she could see that he didn't look right. And not just because he was all broken up.

Oh well, that was for the lab guys to figure out, Terashita thought. You did your job of alleviating the threat. But now you should head up to the roof to see if anyone else needs help.

She began heading towards the hospital entrance when she

sensed someone coming up behind her. She turned to see Officer Parker, one of the younger members of the force.

"Hey, that was really great the way you handled that situation," he said, sounding a bit nervous. "No one else was doing anything, including myself, and you took charge. Way to go."

Terashita blushed slightly. *Finally, some respect. Sure, it's coming from a rookie, but still better than nothing.*

"Thanks, Parker," she said, standing a bit taller. "What do you say you back me up while I head inside and up to the roof."

"Absolutely," the young officer responded, now sounding like the proud one.

The two officers walked together toward the hospital entrance. "By the way," Parker said, "that was pretty hot when you were shooting your gun."

Terashita stopped, put her head in her hand, and rubbed her temples. She sighed and resumed her trek to the hospital entrance.

38

MERRY X-MAS!

In her weakened condition, it wasn't exactly easy pulling Zack fully onto the rooftop. But they had come this far that Samantha wasn't about to let him go now. She found enough strength, along with the little bit of help that Zack could provide himself, to pull him into a less precarious situation.

No longer at risk of falling over the edge, Zack looked down to the street below. It was difficult to see the exact condition of the creature that had been hunting them all night, but it did appear that he now lay in a position that was not conducive to being alive.

Samantha leaned down to look over the edge of the building along with Zack. "He doesn't look good," she said.

"No, he doesn't," Zack stated. "Bad for him, good for us."

"I can't believe this is finally over," Samantha said. "Although I can't believe any of this happened in the first place. I thought for sure we were both dead a couple of times."

"You and me both," Zack replied. "In fact, I think I might *still* be dead. I can't feel anything in my entire body."

"Oh, shit," Samantha said, it suddenly dawning on her that Zack was completely naked laying in the snow. He had already been out in the cold for too long, with only a flimsy hospital gown to protect him. Now with nothing at all, along with all of his other injuries, he needed to get back inside and tended to.

She quickly stood up and pulled her scrubs top over her head, leaving her in just her thermal. She then helped Zack to his feet and slipped the garment over Zack's head and onto his naked, shivering body. Zack was having a lot of trouble staying upright, making it difficult work to get the shirt onto him and keep him on his feet, but she managed.

"It's not much, but better than nothing," she said. The top was large enough that it hung down slightly past Zack's waist, which he was grateful for. Despite everything, he didn't care to have his private parts completely on display.

"Thanks," Zack said through chattering teeth, although Samantha was right. The flimsy garment wasn't providing much comfort from the cold.

"Let's get you inside where we can take care of your properly," Samantha said, wrapping her arm around Zack. She held onto his hand with one of her own, and rubbed his arm with the other, doing her best to create some warming friction.

"Now *that*'s a little better," Zack said, embracing the warmth that Samantha's body was providing. He also couldn't help but notice how her gray thermal clung to her body, something that was much less obvious with the scrubs top covering it.

They began to move toward the shattered doorway. Zack stumbled, but Samantha didn't let him fall. She squeezed his hand and continued massaging his arm as they moved.

"Thanks for risking your life for me back there," Samantha said as they shambled their way forward. "For a minute, I really thought you were a goner."

"No problem," Zack said through still chattering teeth. "That's what I do. Save beautiful women in distress."

"Look at you," Samantha replied. "Still the charmer despite everything."

"Hey, it's not every day that you get attacked by a monstrous Santa Claus beast, nearly fall off of a building, and get to run around with a super hot nurse. And on Christmas Eve no less!"

"Well I appreciate both the life saving and the compliments. And if you really think I'm so hot, as you keep telling me, I'm going to do something else that will make your night." Samantha turned her body so that she faced Zack directly. She looked into his eyes, smiled, and leaned in. Their lips met. They melted into each other, the trauma of the night's events manifesting itself in the kiss.

Samantha pulled away. She looked at Zack again. At first, his eyes remained closed, but he slowly opened them. A smile crept upon his lips.

"Now I *definitely* feel better," he said sleepily.

Samantha laughed. "I'm sure. Now let's get you back inside where we can really take care of you."

Zack's smile grew. "*Really* take care of me? What exactly did you have in mind?"

Samantha laughed again. "Slow down there, champ. We're going to get you the proper medical treatment before anything. Once your back in good health, then we can discuss your reward for saving my life."

"So there *is* a reward? This Christmas is turning around quickly!"

"Perhaps," Samantha said slyly. "Although you're a little younger than my normal type."

"Yeah, well, judging by your last boyfriend, maybe you should deviate from your normal type."

Samantha glared at him, but with no real malice. "True enough," she said. "Although I'm pretty sure there's something in the hand-book about dating your patients."

"After tonight, I think we can throw the handbook out the window," Zack said.

Samantha smiled devilishly at Zack, and with that, she escorted him to and through the doorway and back into the hospital.

ABOUT THE AUTHOR

Eric Blood lives in the Philadelphia suburbs where he loves to read, watch stupid horror movies (and an occasional good one), listen to punk rock, and write sleazy horror stories. His wife, son, and three crazy cats put up with him for some reason.

He is working on creating a somewhat professional looking website, but in the meantime, you can check out his writing updates on Goodreads.

Eric is currently working on his next novel.